THE LAPLANCHE BOYS

NATISHA RAYHOR

Chapter One

The brakes on the train squeaked loudly as it came to a rumbling stop, and Azon was tempted to shoot up out of his seat and make a beeline for the exit before anyone else could do so. He had never ridden on a train before, and the eight-hour trip wasn't something that he was looking forward to ever doing again. Despite being desperate to abandon his seat and get off the train, he remained seated as those around him stood up and wrestled with their suitcases and bags. Azon waited until the aisle was clear before standing up and grabbing the one suitcase that contained everything he brought with him from Orlando, Florida to Diamond Cove, North Carolina.

Azon didn't have a lot, but he'd elected to trash a lot of his clothes and shoes prior to leaving home, promising himself that once he started seeing some money, he'd go shopping. Until then, basketball shorts, sweats, tees, and two pairs of J's would suffice. There were three pairs of jeans and two expensive shirts folded among the items in his suitcase in the event he chose to go somewhere that would require him looking decent, but all Azon had on his mind was money. He was coming to foreign territory with one objective and one objective only. To get money.

His younger brother, Islande, was coming down in a week or so. If it was up to him, he would have been on the train alongside Azon, but Islande was the one that helped their parents run the convenience store they owned. They begged him not to go until they found a replacement. His parents didn't want him to go at all, but Islande and Azon may as well have been twins because even though there was a two-year age difference with twenty-five-year old Azon being the oldest, the brothers were practically joined at the hip. If Azon was there, you could bet Islande was already there or on the way.

Let Medjine and Michael tell it, Islande was their good son, and Azon was the bad apple. It was always Azon doing something devilish, and Islande always tagged along for the ride. Neither parent saw it as honorable when Azon murdered the man that had robbed their store a week earlier and relived them of everything in the register and the store safe which was a little more than $2,000. Never mind that the thief took their mortgage money. Medjine and Michael wanted the police to do their job, find the man, and arrest him. When they heard he'd been gunned down in an alley, they both knew who the culprit was, and Medjine cried for hours wondering what she'd done wrong. How did she end up raising such a savage? She was a God-fearing woman and tried her best to raise her children to be the same way, but Azon didn't fear anything except being broke it seemed.

His cousin, Fabienne couldn't have called at a better time and stated that he'd been released from prison. He wanted Azon and Islande to come to Diamond Cove and hit a few licks with him, and Azon was down. If he was down, then so was Islande. And so it was written. Azon purchased a train ticket, packed everything that he didn't throw away, and he was off. His parents breathed a sigh of relief, while his sister, Angeline cried. She was in college and lived in a dorm, but she saw her brother a few times a month, and they were close. Islande and Angeline understood Azon. He went hard for the people that he loved, and they didn't see anything wrong with it. Their parents, however, feared God's wrath and also man's. They never wanted anyone that Azon had wronged to retaliate against them in any way.

It was Azon's parents that constantly villainized him for not going to college, not having a job, and not being who they wanted him to be. Azon was a get it by any means necessary type of guy and most often his necessary was something violent or illegal. Azon made his way off the train and as soon as he stepped from the train to the sidewalk, his eyes darted around in search of Fabienne. He hadn't seen his cousin in more than five years, but he knew he'd recognize him as soon as he laid eyes on him. Azon had the normal bop of most hood niggas. The Glock tucked securely in his waist and the slight bow of his legs made him walk with his legs slightly further apart than most people.

Azon had just entered the train station when through the large windows, he could see Fabienne leaning up against a black Toyota. The SUV was nice and probably belonged to his aunt Johanne who had a good job working for the state of North Carolina. It was unlikely that Fabienne already had a car after only being home from prison for two days and although it was nice, the vehicle wasn't really Fabienne's style. Azon placed his fist in front of his mouth and grinned wide as he pushed the door open and stepped outside.

"This nigga don' got brolic as fuck," he declared as he eyed Fabienne's muscular frame. His cousin stood 6'2 and had to weigh at least two hundred and seventy pounds. It looked like the nigga lived in the gym. The only past time that Azon had that his parents approved of was boxing, and even with all of the time he spent in the gym, he wasn't as bulked up as Fabienne.

Fabienne's pecan-colored skin was covered in tattoos. He had a low cut and sideburns that connected to a full thick beard.

"They got steroids in the bing, nigga?" Azon joked as Fabienne grinned and gave him dap before pulling him into a brotherly hug.

"Hell nah but in the joint, you either find hobbies, sleep all day, or listen to niggas lie. I wasn't about to sleep for two years, and you already know how I feel about niggas, so I got into working out. A lot."

Azon chuckled as he got into the car. With all the dirt he'd done in his life, he was amazed that he'd never seen the inside of a jail cell. Fabienne caught an assault with a deadly weapon with intent to kill charge for catching a nigga that jumped him and beating him damn near to death with his hands first and then a baseball bat second. Taj had pulled up at his baby mama's house with his cousin, and they caught Fabienne in her bed. The men snuck up on him from behind and not only was Fabienne drunk and caught off guard, but there were two of them, so it was a no win situation. They beat Fabienne so badly that he had to get his jaw wired shut.

He was down bad for almost a month after that incident. His face was so swollen and bruised that he wasn't even recognizable for weeks. Azon wanted to come down then and help his cousin handle his shit, but Fabienne assured him that he had it under control. He ended up seeing Taj two months later at the racetrack, and he went and got his baseball bat out of the car. There was no way he was pulling a gun out in front of hundreds of people, but he'd damn sure beat ass with an audience. He handed the bat to his homeboy to hold while he confronted Taj. Fabienne refused to catch the man off guard. He didn't want to sneak him the way he'd been unexpectedly ambushed. Fabienne wanted to whoop him fair and square, and that's what he did. The same baby mama that Fabienne had slept with was crying and screaming for Fabienne to stop the brutal assault. Without his cousin helping him, Taj didn't have hands and was no match for Fabienne. He knocked Taj to the ground with the third punch, but he continued to beat the man mercilessly. Fabienne wanted to inflict the same pain on him that Taj and his cousin did to him.

By the time he finished beating Taj, the man was unconscious and barely moving, and missing a few teeth. The police had arrived four cars deep. Fabienne didn't even care about being arrested. His only regret was that he didn't get Taj's cousin too. But Fabienne didn't forget shit, and he was confident that he'd get his revenge in due time. Two years later, he still had a grudge, and he had the man's face etched in his mental rolodex even though he didn't even know his name.

As soon as they pulled off from the train station, Fabienne got down to business. "I love my moms, but I'm not trying to stay with her any longer than I have to. We can't wait for Islande to come. I have a lick that I need us to hit immediately. Like tonight. My first day out, I went to the trap and smoked with my boy, and I came up on some shit that's damn near too good to be true."

He grinned, showing off his straight pearly whites while Azon grunted and ran his hand through his wild shoulder-length locs. "You know most of the time when shit is too good to be true, that's because it is," he repeated to Fabienne a saying that his father lived by.

"Check it though," Fabienne began to plead his case. "My man sells heroin. Fiend came to the house and copped $500 worth of dope, and my man was like got damn, Nice you were just here this morning and spent like $300. Who you done robbed? Nice wasn't saying much at first, but he got high, and started running his mouth to a female that he ended up sharing his dope with."

Fabienne's phone rang, and he picked it up from his lap, looked at it, and placed it back down. Ignoring the call, he continued with his story. "I'm outside talking to moms and shit on the phone, but I hear him telling her, that he did construction for some Italian man out in Greensboro, and he broke into the man's house and got like $400,000 out of his safe and some jewelry. He was telling the woman that if she pawned the jewelry for him, he'd give her half the money. We need to go get that money from that nigga before he shoots it all up." Fabienne glanced over at Azon, and Azon saw the gleam in his cousin's eyes.

"The nigga was so high out of his mind, that he didn't even notice that I followed him home. I know where he lives. My first thought was, he's a fuckin' fiend, so I could have run up in his shit right then and there with him being high, but his neighbors were out on the porch. I'm telling you though. Every hour that passes, the more money he puts in his arm. I don't know if he lives alone, and I don't want to risk going in there dolo. I could have asked anyone, but I don't trust anybody like I trust you. Feel me?"

Robbing a fiend sounded like an easy enough lick, so Azon gave a slight nod. "Feel you. Shit, I'm with it." He had no reservations about taking the money from the man that would probably end up overdosing if he kept the money in his possession.

"My nigga," Fabienne smiled ready to get to the money and get back on his shit.

***

Johanne cooked an elaborate meal for Fabienne and Azon, and Azon took a shower and changed clothes after his long train ride. Fabienne was twenty-five and much like Azon, he could have a temperamental side, but his mother only saw the good in him. Before prison, he worked a job as a welder for a few years, and he sold weed on the side. Fabienne had no desire to come home and beg anyone for a job. He was well aware that despite his experience, no one would be jumping to give him a job after he'd just been released from prison for such a violent crime. It didn't matter anyway because even though Fabienne didn't knock a 9-5, he lost a lot when he went away and the quickest way to get it back was with fast money. Before going to prison, he lived in a two bedroom townhouse and drove a Corvette. Once he went away, he lost his car and of course, his lease was broken, so now his credit was bad.

Johanne believed that it would be just that easy for Fabienne to come home and get his life back on track the legitimate way. When he asked to borrow her car, she didn't hesitate to hand over her keys. She didn't hesitate to loan him money or do whatever he asked of her because he was her oldest child and only son, and she'd do anything for him. Johanne was clueless to the fact that her son had invited Azon to Diamond Cove to be his partner in crime. When they got dressed that night, she told them to have fun not knowing that they were going to rob a man.

Fabienne didn't ask to borrow his mother's car, because he didn't want her vehicle associated with the crime that he was about to commit. He and Azon took off walking and once they were two blocks over, Fabienne pulled out his phone and went to a ride share app. The plan was to get dropped off a mile from the fiend's home and to walk the rest of the way. On Fabienne's back was a backpack that contained two pairs of black, leather gloves, duct tape, and all of the tools that he needed to gain entry to the Nice's house, so he wouldn't have to draw unwanted attention to the crime by kicking in the door or breaking glass.

As they waited on the ride, Fabienne ran all of his plans down to Azon. "Once we have money in our possession, we can get on pretty quickly. There are a few more niggas that we can get at. Once we have enough bread, we can cop some dope. This robbing shit is what I'm on for a minute. The money comes faster than having to sit in a trap all day or post up on a block serving fiends. I'm not talking about petty licks either. There's this Asian nigga I want to hit that has an Internet café. It's always big money in that bitch."

"Robbing comes with more risks," Azon stated as the Uber approached. "I mean, I'm with whatever, 'cus I have $500 to my name, and I'll rob a muhfucka before I'm walking around broke, but robbing is far from easy. There's a lot of risks associated with it," he reiterated the part about the risks because he felt he couldn't stress it enough.

"There's risk associated with everything. I just know with me, you, and Islande, we can hit some heavy licks. From there, it's up."

Azon simply nodded as he got into the back of the Uber because he didn't need much convincing. He didn't come all the way to North Carolina to get locked up or killed, but he didn't come to be broke either. Fabienne knew the area, and he knew more about the people than Azon did, so Azon had no issues following his lead. What he and Fabienne had in common the most was the trust factor. If their life or freedom was on the line, Azon knew without a shadow of a doubt that he could count on Islande and Fabienne in a way he'd never put his trust in anyone else. When it came to committing crimes, Azon either did it with his brother and cousin or alone. He didn't even hit licks with his best friend, Alpha.

A thought occurred to Azon while they were on their way to their destination. "What happened to that broad you were dealing with?" He turned towards Fabienne. "Kourtney or some shit."

"Khloe. I still rock with her, but I'm fresh out. Money is the main thing on my mind. Pussy is running a close second, but I'm not really up for the headache that comes with being attached. If I have to run the streets from sun up 'til sun down to get to the money, that's what I'm gon' do. I'm not going to be answering my phone every two seconds to be questioned and treated like I'm on probation. She thought I was coming home to move in with her, and that's a hell no. I want my own spot."

"I feel you on that. You got me bringing Islande, so I know you know we're going to need a spot. I hope you have some plugs and connections on the private landlords, and we don't want to live in the hood."

Azon's parents owned a convenience store, and his father had a small landscaping business. Michael was a very hardworking and humble man, and he didn't believe in living above his means. When he first came to the states from Haiti when Azon was four, and Islande was two, he moved his family into the hood where they lived for almost ten years. When Azon was thirteen, his father put $25,000 down on a $150,000 house in a decent enough neighborhood, and they moved into the modest three-bedroom home.

Once they were away from the hood and Azon's school district changed, he continued to keep in touch with his old friends as well as make new ones. He wasn't the friendliest person in the world, but people tended to gravitate towards him. He became popular and was soon, 'good in any hood.' It didn't matter what side of town it was on, Azon traveled alone most times, and no one ever really tried him. There were parts of Florida that were so gritty, it wasn't recommended for tourists to venture there, and Azon was comfortable in those parts because he knew the laws of the land. Though he was comfortable in the hoods of Florida, he didn't know a thing about Diamond Cove, and he refused to lay his head in the hood.

"You know I got you covered. My mom's landlord has plenty of houses, and a few of them are empty. My mom has been renting from her for six years and has never been late paying the rent. She always gives compliments on how clean my mom keeps the house, and she's never had any complaints. She's even talking about letting my mom start some rent to own shit. She'll rent to you just off the strength of my mom's name. She knows me too, and she remembers when I was a welder. You know moms ran the story down about my assault charge and let it be known that I was the victim, so I'm good too." Fabienne smiled wide, and Azon chuckled.

Anyone that knew them knew that Johanne was going to take up for Fabienne right or wrong. Where Azon's parents never missed a chance to blame him for some shit, Johanne stood ten toes down for Fabienne, and he ate that shit up. He was a mama's boy to the core. The driver pulled up to the destination, and the men got out of the car. Simultaneously, they pulled ski masks from their pockets and placed them on their heads. No one was out and aside from a few dogs barking the neighborhood was pretty quiet. When the men came up on the house, Fabienne slid the straps of the bookbag off his shoulders and walked around into the back yard. He placed the gloves on his hands and quietly pulled the screen door open.

While Fabienne used a screwdriver and an old debit card to gain entry into the house, Azon screwed the silencer onto his Glock. Fabienne had the door open in less than five minutes, and the men eased inside the home. There were no lights on in the kitchen, but the television in the living room was playing, and a faint light illuminated the room just enough for the men to make their way through.

Fabienne led the way and with his finger caressing the trigger of his gun, he crept into the living room as he pulled his ski mask down over his face, and Azon followed suit. The living room was empty. The men made their way down the dark hallway, and Fabienne twisted the doorknob on the first room they came to. He pushed the door open and the night light that was plugged in by the door allowed him to see the small body of a child underneath the covers on a twin sized bed.

"Merde," he cursed underneath his breath in French. Fabienne looked over his shoulder at Azon. "There's a kid in there, but they're asleep. Let's make this shit quick."

The house only had two bedrooms and as soon as the pair reached the second door the sound of a bed knocking into the wall cut through the silence in the home.

"Fuck me, Nice! Yes, baby, just like that!"

Fabienne shook his head as the shrills from the loud ass female drifted into the hallway. He wasn't sure who all lived in the house, but he assumed she knew there was a child asleep right in the next room. Fabienne entered the dark room with Azon on his heels and immediately he gagged at the foul odor permeating through the air.

'Ain't no way they in here fucking smelling like that' Azon thought as the foul stench smacked him in the nose even though his face was covered with a mask.

Fabienne moved his hand around the wall until he found the light switch. The moment light filled the room, Nice stopped mid-stroke and jumped up to see who was in the room while the woman he was sexing screamed.

"Shut the fuck up," Azon growled as he pointed a gun at them while looking over his shoulder to make sure the noise didn't draw the child from his or her room.

Nice's eyes were glossed over, but he wasn't so high that he wasn't aware of what was going on. His heart dropped at the thought of the men taking his money. The day he robbed his old boss, he was about to get evicted. He paid the two months' rent that he was behind, paid the rent for the upcoming month, got the lights turned back on, bought some food, and he had been shooting up the rest. Nice was in dope fiend heaven with his never-ending supply of cash. He had even purchased a car earlier. Nice had already run through about $20,000, and it had only been a few days. He had quickly become a favorite among the neighborhood dope boys because he was blessing their pockets heavily.

"Sit down," Fabienne demanded. Fiends were tricky, and he didn't trust Nice to wait patiently while he searched the house. The man would try something for sure, and Fabienne didn't want to have to kill him, so he was going to tape his ankles and hands together. He didn't mind putting his robbery game down, but he was trying to avoid catching bodies if possible.

"Come on, man. I don't have nothing. Why you up in my shit? I'm just a junkie. I don't have shit man." He was on the verge of tears because for the first time ever, he didn't have to wake up every morning and scheme and plot to get high. He had money and drugs at his disposal, and he was able to stay high around the clock.

"I don't like repeating myself," Fabienne stated in a calm tone. He was going to give the man two seconds to cooperate.

By the time he took a few strides across the room, Nice was still standing in the same spot, so Fabienne hit him so hard that the man fell back into the wall. He was asleep before his body even hit the floor. Fabienne's eyes fell on a pile of money that was on the nightstand next to a bag of heroine, and he placed the money in the bookbag. Azon remained by the door with his gun trained on the crying woman as Fabienne opened drawers, went in the closet and searched through shoe boxes, and even looked underneath the stained mattress. There was money poorly hidden all over the room and when he was satisfied, Fabienne nodded at Azon, and they turned to leave the room. The woman was still in the bed with her knees drawn to her chest crying, while Nice was laid out on the floor snoring.

A startled Azon jumped and pointed his gun when he stepped into the hallway and was met by a figure. It didn't take him long to realize that the person standing in the hallway was a child, and she didn't know how close she'd come to being shot. Azon hated playing a part in possibly traumatizing a child, but with addicts for parents, she was probably already fucked up anyway. He and Fabienne rushed past her and left the house.

"Told you that shit was gon' be easy," Fabienne declared as they ran three blocks over.

When they felt they were far enough away, the men stopped running and began walking down the street. Fabienne pulled his phone from his pocket to request an Uber. Azon kept his eyes on their surroundings. This was the hood, so he knew police didn't care about the residents being victims of crimes, but they could possibly be patrolling the area hoping to catch some criminals in the act. It wasn't about keeping the neighborhood safe but more about getting niggers off the street. If the police pulled up on them with a bookbag full of money, their asses would be grass. Azon was prepared to haul ass if need be. Hell, he might even shoot it out with the police, but going to jail wasn't in his plans for the night.

Fabienne's phone was constantly vibrating as he requested a ride. He kissed his teeth and shook his head. "See what I mean? Khloe has called me four times in ten minutes. When I finally talk to her, she's going to swear I'm with a female."

All Azon cared about was counting the money they had acquired. His right hand was itching for that shit. It only took the Uber four minutes to come, and the men rode in silence all the way back to Johanne's house. Inside Fabienne's room with the door locked, the men counted $380,000. Azon had never in his life held that much money in his hands at once. When Fabienne handed him his cut which was $190,000, Azon finally began to breathe easy. If this was an indication of how good North Carolina was going to be to him, then he couldn't wait to get shit cracking.

Chapter two

"Why you sitting over there with a long face?" Gia's father asked her as he cut into his steak.

Gia sipped her water through a straw and placed the glass back on the table. She hated having to talk about her relationship issues with her father because he never missed a chance to throw it up in her face that he told her not to talk to Money in the first place. Gia was real tired of being reminded of the fact that her father was against her dating Money in the beginning. Gia met money two years ago because her father was his manager. Money was a boxer, and Gia's father, Blake, was a retired boxer. He saw Money's potential, took him under his wing, and started training and managing him.

Money and Gia snuck around at first, but the situation became hard to hide and when Blake found out, he was livid. He had lived the life before, and he knew that Money was too young, had too many goals, and was coming into too much money to be in a relationship with anyone let alone his baby girl. Blake was against the relationship for many reasons. The first one being that he didn't want Money to become lovesick and get knocked off his square. He needed the young man focused and winning fights. A woman could be a man's biggest distraction if he didn't have the right mindset. The second reason he didn't want them dating was of course because Gia was his daughter. She was literally his twin from her light skin and thick curly hair down to the freckles that decorated her nose.

If Money dealt with groupies or did anything to hurt Gia, Blake knew it would piss him off. He wasn't trying to mix business with the personal like that, but

Gia fought him tooth and nail on it. She even went as far as moving out of his house and moving in with Money. Gia and her father didn't speak for four months, but he finally came around. He made it clear to her that she was grown, it was her life, and whatever Money did, he didn't want to hear shit about it.

For the past seven months, Gia had been going through, and it was becoming hard to pretend that she was happy when she wasn't. Because of her almost constant sullen moods, she stayed away from her family as much as possible, but that made her even more miserable because she'd always been close with her parents and her sister, Kaylin.

"I'm fine, daddy. I'm just tired. I had to fire someone yesterday, and another girl quit today. Running your own business isn't all people think it's cracked up to be," she pouted as she speared a scalloped potato with her fork. Her clothing store was stressing her out, but that wasn't the reason she was sad. She'd never admit that she was pissed because Money had stayed out until six AM. He was getting real bold with the disrespect, and Gia was tired of it. She'd *been* tired of it.

"I know all about that," he grunted. "But there are always people looking for jobs, so replacing them shouldn't be too hard. Just hang in there. Be thorough with your hiring process, and only hire dependable, mature people."

Gia nodded as she placed a piece of steak into her mouth.

"You coming to the fight Friday night?" he eyed her intensely to see how she'd react to the mention of the fight. Blake wasn't stupid, and he knew that Gia and Money had been into it lately. He'd been having to dig into Money's ass too much for his game being off.

When Money first started training, he used to listen. While training for a fight, Blake always suggested no sex, no alcohol, no weed, no social media, no distractions. As time went on and Money got richer and became big-headed, he felt he didn't have to follow Blake's advice. He'd hang out all night partying and drinking then come in the gym, and be so off his game that you could practically see steam coming out of Blake's ears. It took him losing one match to get his shit together. But Blake could tell when Money and Gia were into it because not only would Money be off, but Gia's mood would be sour as well.

"Yeah, I'll be there," she replied with fake enthusiasm.

"Good. What about you, Kaylin? You coming out to the fight?"

Being that their father used to be a boxer, his daughters had a love for the sport even though he was retired. "No, I can't make this one. I have clinicals on Saturday, and I have to get up at like four in the morning, so I can be there at six. It's about thirty minutes away from my apartment." Kaylin was almost done with school and about to become a dental hygienist.

When dinner was finished, Gia and Kaylin helped their mother clean the kitchen, and she kissed her parents and sister goodbye before heading out to her Kia. The entire sixteen minute drive to Money's townhouse, Gia was in a zone. She had really become *that* girl. She didn't have actual proof that Money was cheating, but a lot of his actions were suspect as fuck. And honestly, if he wasn't cheating, they still had problems. He was giving outside forces way more attention than he was giving his girl, and Gia was no longer happy. She couldn't even remember the last time he'd taken her out on a date or on vacation, but he made time for his boys no matter the circumstances.

Gia had her own clothing boutique, and it kept her pretty busy. Even if she had two salespeople on the schedule, she often stopped by her store because it was her baby. She was right there putting in work, dressing the mannequins, putting out inventory, dealing with returns, etc. Most weeks, she went to her boutique seven days a week, and she stayed no less than six hours each time. Gia started out selling only women's clothing, accessories, and shoes, but she now had a side for the men. Her father had given her the money to invest in quality merchandise, so the clothes weren't cheap. Men and women alike shopped in her store, and Gia was seeing very good money.

She wasn't rich, however, and she knew if it wasn't for Money, she might be struggling just a little bit. The month before, her profit after she paid the store bills, paid her employees, etc. was $4,000. That was pretty good, but these days the rent on a decent place was damn near $2,000 a month. She wouldn't be balling off $4,000 a month if she were single, but since she lived with Money and he paid all the bills, she was straight.

Gia pulled up to their three-bedroom townhouse and parked beside Money's BMW truck. With his 6'3 frame, cashew-colored skin and body full of colorful tattoos, Gia was smitten with her man. His physique was sick, and he loved eating pussy. He had a great career, his sex game was on point, and he was fine. If he was trying to finish the way he started, Gia wouldn't have any complaints. Back when Blake was against their relationship, Money would text Gia long ass paragraphs, professing his love for her. He'd let her know how deeply he loved her, and how nothing would keep him away from her. He planned romantic getaways and sent her flowers for no reason.

Now, all of that had changed. He hadn't done anything romantic for her in months. He rarely texted her unless he was asking her to cook his favorite meal, pick his clothes up from the cleaners, or begging her to find something that he misplaced. The honeymoon phase was over, and Gia missed it desperately. Maybe he would come around, or maybe he wouldn't. She walked into the lavishly decorated townhouse and took her shoes off at the door. Gia walked up the stairs and when she entered the bedroom, she found Money in bed snoring. Being that he had a fight coming up, he had super early mornings, so him being asleep this early wasn't uncommon.

Gia leaned up against the doorframe and watched her man as he slept in the bed. She loved Money wholeheartedly, but love wasn't enough. Gia wasn't happy anymore, and she had expressed that to Money several times. The thing that hurt her was that he didn't seem interested in making her happy. She told him time and time again what he needed to change in order for her to be happy, and he wasn't making the moves to do those things. Gia didn't know how much more she could take, and that alone broke her heart.

***

The next day, Money woke up on the right side of the bed. By the time he was finished with his morning workout, Gia was up and cooking him breakfast. He convinced her to go to the boutique later in the day, so she could accompany him to the gym for practice. One would have thought that he invited her to a sunset dinner on the beach. Gia was flattered that he wanted to spend time with her, so she got dressed in black Nike leggings and a matching sports bra. She brushed her thick curls up into a bun and lined her lips with her favorite red liner and filled her lips in with matte red gloss. Her face was bare, but her juicy lips were popping. Gia rarely wore foundation because she didn't like hiding her freckles, so she always made sure her lashes and lips were on point. She turned around, stood on her tip toes, and admired her booty in the mirror. Being with a boxer had its' perks because Money often trained her, and Gia's 5'7 frame was sick. She had the booty that women paid for and the thighs to match.

Gia eyed the $5,000 Van Cleef bracelet on her wrist. It was a Valentine's Day gift that came in the mail a month ago. She loved the bracelet but not the way she received it. She would have loved to have had a romantic dinner with her man for Valentine's Day, but he spent the entire day training and was too tired to go out when he was done. He came home and made her aware that the package that had been delivered was hers, and he went to take a shower while she opened it. He really made Gia question her sanity. Was she doing too much? Should she just be satisfied that she got a gift and not care that the gesture wasn't romantic?

Gia settled into the passenger side of her man's whip and ordered inventory for the boutique on her phone as he drove towards the gym.

"I was thinking this year for my birthday, that I want to go to London." Money's voice broke into her thoughts. "Cease said he wants to go too, so I think that will be a dope ass guy's trip."

Gia whipped her head in his direction and narrowed her eyes. "For your birthday, you want to go out of the country with niggas?" She was offended, and she didn't care if he knew it.

Money could see the attitude that was written all over her face. Her button nose was turned up, Gia's eyes were narrowed, and she had frown lines in her forehead. He groaned. "Don't tell me that's a problem. Yo have I ever had an issue with you going on a girl's trip?"

"I don't care." Gia's voice cracked, and that infuriated her even more. She hated the fact that she cried when she was angry because it made her feel weak. She hated crying. "We haven't been on a vacation in months. You didn't even do anything with me on Valentine's Day. You think I don't want to go to London? Now, you're sitting here telling me you're going on a guy's trip? That's suspect as fuck."

"Suspect?" Money's voice rose an octave. "Yo don't use that word when you're describing me."

Gia kissed her teeth and frowned. "No one is talking about your sexuality! But it seems that you want to spend time with everyone except me. What changed? We used to stay going on trips and dates."

Her facial muscles relaxed, and pain filled her eyes. Just that fast she'd gone from being angry to being hurt. Money kissed his teeth. "I have a fight coming up in a few days, and you want to be stressing me out over dumb shit. You're not my trainer. You don't help me prepare for fights, but didn't I invite you with me today? But I don't want to spend time with you?"

Money was now the one raising his voice and frowning, and Gia's heart rate increased. This was what she hated. Money always made her question her feelings. She would start out feeling strongly about an issue and in the end, he'd always make her feel like maybe she was tripping and doing the most. She didn't want to stress him out before his fight, and she didn't want him to regret inviting her to the gym. She loved spending time with him. Gia decided to just push the London trip to the back of her mind and not mention it again until after his match. If he lost this fight, her father would be pissed, and Money would be super pissed. The last thing she needed was for it to be deemed her fault.

The rest of the ride was quiet and filled with tension. At the gym, Gia walked in behind Money and tried to keep her emotions at bay. She got tired of walking around pretending that nothing was wrong when she was hurt or angry or feeling disrespected. Money had started to make her feel like all she did was nag and create problems, and she began to believe it. Gia had no desire to be in a relationship where she didn't even feel comfortable expressing herself, but she couldn't leave Money alone. She loved him. He was her drug.

Money found his trainer, William, and approached him. He gave William dap and placed his bag on the floor.

"Hey, Gia, boo." William gave her a one-armed hug, and she gave him a small smile.

Gia sat down in one of the metal folding chairs that sat against the wall, and she watched Money intently. If he didn't do good in the ring, she'd know that she really did have the ability to stress him out and throw him off his game. No matter how important she wanted to be to him, she knew she'd never be more important than boxing. Gia had no desire to affect his game in a negative way, so she told herself that until this match was over, she wouldn't argue with him about anything.

Money and William started off sparring, and he looked good to her. Money was damn near undefeated. He lost one fight and that wasn't even because his opponent was a better boxer than him. Money had just done too much the night before, and he boxed terribly due to having a hangover and a headache. That was a big no no, and Blake tore into him so bad that you couldn't pay Money to drink alcohol the week of a match let alone the night before. He was young and bullheaded, but he was starting to really take his career seriously. The money for the matches was steadily increasing, and he was getting endorsements. Money's net worth was climbing by the night, and he didn't want to mess that up. Every win he got in the ring was a win for his brand.

Instincts made Gia look up and when she did, she locked eyes with a man that took her breath away. He stood around 6'2 with pecan-colored skin and thick wicks in his hair. Some people looked down on those kinds of locs, but they made Gia's pussy wet. Dread head bit his bottom lip slightly showing off the gold teeth in his mouth, and Gia had to squeeze her thighs together because her yoni was contracting violently. The fact that she was lusting over this rugged ass work of art while her man was a few feet away was insane.

The man had a lean build, but she could tell he was athletic for sure. His muscles weren't bulging like the man that he was with, but Gia was willing to bet money that he donned a six-pack underneath the white tee that he wore. Tattoos adorned his arms, and his almond-shaped eyes were one of his best features. Gia's face flushed with embarrassment as he chucked his chin up at her. She looked away quickly and focused her attention back on her man. Out of her peripheral vision, she could see that the men had stopped walking, and she prayed that the one she'd been ogling had the good sense not to approach her. Money may have been slacking on showing her attention, but he hated when other men did it.

Gia nervously glanced in the direction of the men, and she breathed a sigh of relief when she saw that they were watching Money. Mr. Wicks tapped his friend's chest with the back of his hand and said something and they both laughed. *Jesus, he's even sexier when he laughs*. Gia wasn't sure what had come over her, but she'd never lusted over a man that hard while she was with Money. In her eyes, there wasn't a man walking this earth that was better than her man, but this man had her thinking real different.

Money took a break and walked over to the ropes. He removed his mouth piece with an agitated glare at his girl wondering why she wasn't waiting with his bottle of water in hand. He didn't even have to open his mouth. Just seeing the irritation on his face, snapped Gia out of the trance that she was in, and she jumped up and went over to his bag. Gia handed her man the bottle of water and as he guzzled it down, something in the opposite direction had his attention. Gia followed his gaze, and Mr. Wicks was in the ring with the guy he'd come in with, and he was nice. They weren't even fighting for real but his form, and the speed of his hands made it known that he knew what he was doing when it came to boxing. He even had Money's attention. The more he threw jabs and uppercuts, the more aroused Gia became. She didn't want to stare because she knew that was disrespectful to her man, but she couldn't look away.

"You like what you see?" Money's voice cut into her thoughts, and her head snapped in his direction.

"What do you mean?" she asked calmly appearing cool on the outside, but her heart was racing. He had caught her staring.

"I mean you looking real damn hard. Do you like what you see?" Money's nostrils flared, and Gia drew back pretending to be offended.

"I saw you watching, so I looked to see what had your attention. I watched them for two seconds. His form is nice. You forgot that I'm a lover of the sport and not just because you participate in it?"

"Yeah okay," he stated before putting his mouthpiece back in.

Money was possessive and jealous when it came to Gia but for some reason, she felt like her staring wasn't the only reason that he was agitated. They didn't know this man. They'd never seen him in the gym before, and Money doubted he was a professional boxer. But that didn't matter. They only had to watch him for a minute to see that he was a problem in the ring. In a matter of seconds, Mr. Wicks had everyone's attention, and they were marveling over his skills. Gia knew Money well enough to know that he felt threatened. In more ways than one.

Chapter three

"So, what's been up with you?" Gia's best friend Havanna asked as Gia got into Havanna's Jeep Cherokee. Havanna was a nurse, and she had a pretty hectic schedule, so the friends hadn't spoken or talked in a few days and for them, that may as well have been a few months. Havanna was accompanying Gia to Money's fight.

After months of complaining, Gia had started keeping her problems with Money to herself because the more she complained without doing anything about it, it made her feel pathetic. Why keep singing the same sad songs and putting up with the bullshit if she wasn't going to leave or demand that he change? She hadn't vented to Havanna in months, but she had some shit to get off her chest.

"Do you know this man told me that he wants to go on a guy's trip to London for his birthday?"

Havanna turned her head in friend's direction and stared at her.

Gia raised her brows and shook her head signaling Havanna to say something.

"I'm waiting for you to add some mo' shit 'cus what you said didn't make sense," she frowned. "I've heard of guy's trips, but London? With your niggas? Something in the water ain't clean. I see that light-skinned nigga still trying to play in your face."

Gia sighed. She almost wanted Havanna to tell her that she was tripping but if her friend agreed that she wasn't, Gia knew she had to do something about it, and that what's she was dreading. She was so tired of arguing with Money. Why couldn't he just get his shit together for the sake of their relationship?

"He said I was tripping."

"That's what a fuck nigga gon' say. Every time. Stop letting that man play with you and then act like you're crazy for speaking on it."

"He did make a valid point, though. He said he wouldn't trip if I went on a girl's trip."

Havanna exhaled a deep sigh mixed with a groan. "And you don't bitch when he travels with his buddies, but this is his birthday, and he's not going to Miami or Vegas, he's going to London! Who goes on that kind of trip with their homies and not their significant other? It's just weird to me. If I'm in a relationship, we can either do a group trip for my birthday where my man comes along, or me and my man take a trip, and if I want to do something separate with my girls I can. I'm not that single friend that's gon' constantly throw salt on your relationship. When you're happy, I'm happier. But if you have a problem with this, I'm just here to reassure you that no matter what that man says, you aren't tripping."

Gia gave a slight nod. She had so desperately wanted someone to vent to but when the time came, the conversation left her with a heavy heart. Havanna could feel the sadness oozing off of her friend, and she glanced in her direction.

"Chin up, friend. We're not letting that man sour our mood. I finally have four days off after working like a slave for a month. The days are reserved for my daughter, and the nights are reserved for the turn up," she grinned.

Even though Gia was staring down at her feet and not looking at her friend, she could hear the excitement in Havanna's voice, and that made her smile. Gia lifted her head and locked eyes with her friend.

"I could use a good turn up."

"That's what I'm talking about." Gia danced in her seat making Gia laugh.

Gia and Havanna met three years before when Gia was in college. She graduated from Clark Atlanta University with a degree in business. When Gia and Havanna met and realized they were both from Diamond Cove, North Carolina, they clicked instantly. Havanna was a 5'2 ball of fire. With skin the color of the sand in the desert, high cheekbones, and a sharp nose, she had a regal look about her. Havanna was in college to pursue her nursing dreams, and she had no plans of letting getting pregnant at eighteen stop her.

Havanna worked her entire pregnancy and when she left Diamond Cove at seven months pregnant to attend school, she was able to move into a small one bedroom apartment. Her mother came to stay with Havanna for a month when Kendall was born, and Havanna was able to fall into a routine of being a mother and a student. She used her income tax money to pay bills and pay for Kendall to go to daycare. There were even times she had to send Kendall to North Carolina with her mom for a week or two, so she could work every free moment that she had. But with the help of her mother, Havanna made it work, and she walked across that stage with a 4.0 GPA.

Once Havanna and Gia became close, Gia would often come over and watch Kendall so Havanna could go to work or do her homework. Gia's father had money, so her parents didn't want her to work. They wanted her to concentrate on her studies and maintain good grades, so she had no problem with helping her friend out. Havanna was the kind of person that never forgot who had her back when times got tough and from the moment they both moved back to Diamond Cove they continued to be thick as thieves. Havanna was small and petite, but she loved the hips and ass that her daughter had given her, so she had been doing squats, lunges, and other glute enhancing exercises ever since her six week check-up, and people often wondered how she was so small and petite dragging all that ass behind her without having ever laid on a surgeon's table. There were times when her eating habits and hectic schedule caused her to gain a few pounds around the middle, but Havanna didn't care about a pudge as long as that ass was assing.

"I want to go to the racetrack tomorrow night. Nyron is going to be out there on his bike, and you know I love me a man on a motorcycle," she smiled coyly.

The racetrack in Diamond Cove on a Saturday night could be super lit. Gia hadn't been in months. Havanna had a hectic work life and her sister, Kaylin was a student with a boyfriend and clinicals. When they were too busy to hang out, Gia simply stayed at home watching TV and scrolling social media waiting for the moment that her man would show her some attention. Getting out didn't seem like a bad idea. She was tired of sitting in the house like an old maid while life passed her by.

"Sounds like a plan to me. Money's next fight isn't for another seven weeks, so I already know he's going to spend at least two weeks hanging out, drinking, and doing what he wants. I bet none of those nights will include date nights either," she responded dryly.

Havanna shook her head. "It's been a while since I've been in a relationship, but the point of having a man is to have something to do. You don't have to be with him every minute of every day, but if you spend every night bored while he spends every night doing everything except giving you time and attention, that's a problem, Love. A big one."

Gia felt that heaviness again, and she made an internal vow not to bring her relationship up again. It dampened the moment every time. Gia didn't want to keep thinking about how much of a shit show her relationship was let alone talking about it. Havanna pulled up at the venue, and Gia checked her appearance before getting out of the car. That morning, she got a lash fill, and she got knotless box braids that she adored. The braids made her look like a teenager fresh out of high school despite her being a grown woman. Gia hoped that her black remained uncracked for the rest of her life.

The women got nachos, hot dogs, chips, and drinks before finding their front row seats. Gia was nervous because despite her and Money's issues, she wanted the best for him and his career. She wanted him to gain the title of heavyweight champion and go on to be one of the greats. She had prayed long and hard before leaving the house that he would win this fight.

"The boys are out," Havanna sang looking around at the crowd. "Oh shit," she whispered with wide eyes, and her head snapped in Gia's direction. "Is that Lil' Durk?"

Gia strained her neck to see and sure enough walking with four men and his girlfriend, India, the crew was headed in their direction. "Yeah that's him." Gia was eyeing India harder than she was Lil' Durk, and it wasn't because she was gay. Gia could simply appreciate a stunning woman with her shit together. She loved a bossed up, gorgeous, bourgeois black woman.

"I definitely have to come to more of these. I don't know if I'll find my future husband at a boxing match, but I'm sure I could find a good time at one."

Gia chuckled and took a big bite of her hotdog at the very moment that she locked eyes with *him*. Her heart slammed into her ribcage as she eyed Mr. Wicks. Gia had no clue why this man had the ability to stall her breathing and make her heart beat all out of rhythm. She didn't even know him and more importantly, she had a man.

Gia quickly looked away as she grabbed a napkin to wipe her mouth. In a room full of men dressed in designer clothes and shoes and rocking enough ice to light the room, he was the only one that stood out to her, and he managed to do so by rocking a simple pair of dark denim jeans, a red tee shirt with black writing on it, and red and black sneakers. Aside from the watch on his wrist, he donned no jewelry. So simple and basic yet so got damn fine. Gia's mouth was literally watering, and it had nothing to do with the hot dog she was eating.

Gia's gaze was lowered, so she peeped the black and red shoes walk by. A masculine scent wafted into her nostrils as he passed. "Damn they fine as hell," Havanna mumbled, and Gia knew she had to be referring to Mr. Wicks and his friend. The muscular guy with the beard was fine as hell too, but he didn't make Gia's heart beat wildly in her chest the way Mr. Wicks did. Gia finished off her hot dog and guzzled down some Coke as the event started. Havanan and Gia conversed during the undercard fights. When it was time for the main event, a huge smile spread across Gia's face as her man came out to King Von and Lil' Durk's song, *Evil Twin*. The crowd went crazy, and she had to be proud of her man even if things weren't all good at home. She was still rooting for him, and everyone around her knew it from the way she screamed and clapped for him.

Gia saw her father watching intensely from the corner of the ring. The match hadn't even started, and he was still serious as ever with a focused glaze in his eyes. Gia knew at that moment all her father saw was Money. All he was focused on was what Money was about to do in that ring. Money's opponent was announced, and Gia sized him up. He was a muscular white boy with reddish-blonde hair.

"Vanilla Ice is fine as hell," Havanna nudged Gia making Gia laugh.

"Are you in heat?"

"Hell yeah," Havanna replied with no shame in her game making Gia cackle even louder.

The fight started, and from the first punch it was intense. Gia bit her bottom lip furiously as she noticed Money's hands. His right hand was held out too far to the side before and after his jabs making it too easy for his opponent to hit him with a counter jab. *Fix that hand*, Gia willed inwardly just as the white boy delivered a jab that seemed to daze Money for a bit.

"Shit," she hissed underneath her breath.

There was a break, and Gia saw Blake going in. She knew he was chastising Money about the way he was holding his hands. Gia knew if Money lost that match she'd have to avoid him and her father for a few days because they'd be in terrible moods. The break was over, and Gia clapped and cheered trying to offer her man all of the encouragement that she could. The match was intense. There were several moments that Gia held her breath while her eyes bulged out, and her heart raced. All of the makings of a good fight. Gia's nerves were on a hundred, because White Boy had some skills but in the end, Money won. Gia hopped to her feet and cheered and clapped until her hands hurt. When the match was over, Gia and Havanna headed to her Jeep. Gia knew that Money wasn't coming straight home, so she agreed to go get drinks with Havanna.

"Ou' allons nous maintenant."

Gia looked in the direction of the male voice that was speaking French. Once again for the third time that week, she locked eyes with Mr. Wicks, and her face flushed from embarrassment as he smirked at her. He spoke French?! Yes, her panties were officially wet, and she had no clue what he'd even said. It didn't matter. The foreign language sounded so sexy falling off his lips. Gia fantasied about the mystery man speaking French in her ear while he stroked her walls, and her knees almost buckled. She had no idea who this sexy man was, where he'd come from, or why she kept seeing him all of a sudden, but she didn't like it. The way he made her body react was the same ways Money had her in the beginning. Gia wasn't blind, and she could appreciate a fine man, but she was downright lusting after this man. What had gotten into her?

***

"Is that, that nigga, Islande?" Azon asked with a wide grin as he gave his brother dap.

As a grown man, Azon hated to think that he couldn't live his life without *anyone*, but the sigh of relief he breathed when he saw his brother made him aware that he could never comfortably be too far away from Islande. But he was almost certain that the feeling was mutual.

"In the flesh baby," Islande's grin was equally as wide. At 6'1 he was just a hair shorter than his brother. He had the same lean but muscular frame, and he had short locs that he'd just started four months before. He joked that the slight gap between his front teeth is what made him unique because Islande and Azon looked so much alike that people used to mistake them for twins.

Fabienne gave Islande a homeboy hug before Islande got into the backseat of the Charger that Fabienne had rented. Azon wanted to hit one more lick before he purchased a car of his own. He and Fabienne mostly made moves together, but being that Azon was about to move into his own spot, he needed his own vehicle. He wasn't going to put a rental car in his own name, and Johanne had already promised to sign for Fabienne, so Azon was going to ask Fabienne's sister, Jeanne to put a vehicle in her name. Having a lady friend came with perks that didn't just include sex. Azon was going to have to find a female friend or two ASAP, so they could get cars, houses, etc. in their names for him.

When thinking about the fact that he needed a female companion or two, Azon's mind traveled back to thoughts of the sexy woman he kept running into. He saw her the first day he went into the gym to spar with Fabienne, and she was fine indeed. Azon meant no disrespect when he imagined her thick, pink, kissable lips wrapped around his tool. Azon peeped the lame ass nigga that she was with, and he was indifferent. He wasn't that much of a fucked up person to try to holler at her when she was with her man. He felt that would have been out of pocket, but he was battling with himself to leave well enough alone.

If he was in a relationship, men could look all they wanted. He might even give them a pass if they stepped to his shorty because if she didn't shut him down in a way that made him feel stupid for even trying her, then his problem would be with his girl and not the nigga. But if a man was downright coming at his girl knowing that Azon was in the picture it might get ugly. Azon always kept that in mind when approaching a woman. He didn't have a pussy bone in his body, but beefing over women wasn't something that he chose to engage in. Still though...something was telling him that Money nigga didn't know what to do with sexy lips.

The day that Azon went to the gym to spar, he was just fucking around. He wasn't even taking the exercise serious, and he was still aware that all eyes in the gym had been on him. People had been marveling over his boxing skills since the first time he stepped in the ring at ten years old. It all came naturally to him and when it came to boxing, Azon was a very quick learner. It broke the hearts of a few people that he chose running the streets over pursuing boxing on a serious level.

Azon wasn't a hater, so he had no problem admitting that Money had skills. He wasn't a slouch by far, but he couldn't see Azon's hands, and Azon would bet his last dollar on that. Hell, if that nigga was almost undefeated, he knew damn well he'd be undefeated, and that wasn't being cocky. Azon simply knew what he knew.

"What's up? I know y'all niggas sitting on a money making scheme, 'cus I'm ready to get to it. I see you already renting cars and shit, so you must be on to something." Islande spoke up from the backseat.

"Funny you should ask," Fabienne grinned as his orbs lifted to eye Islande through the rearview mirror. "There are some Asians that own an Internet Café. They have cameras, and they have a security guard that's licensed to carry, so we have to be really careful running up in that bitch. But if we can run up in there and lay everybody down, I know we should come out with enough money to make that shit worth the effort."

Azon stared out of the window as he let Fabienne's words sink in. Taking the money from Nice had been like taking candy from a baby, but Azon refused to keep believing that everyone they attempted to rob would be that easy to take from. He wasn't scary. He was smart. He wasn't trying to end up in a jam. He also knew Islande would follow his lead, and he didn't want to lead his brother into some bullshit.

"Y'all with it?" Fabienne looked over at Azon after noticing that he and Islande were pretty quiet.

"I'm with it, but you know robbing niggas and running up in places of business are two different things. You adamant as hell about this jack boy shit. If we pull this lick off, I'd rather just get a pack and get off that shit. All this robbing isn't going to keep going smoothly. I never minded playing with fire, but I also know when to chill. Feel me?"

"I feel you. I definitely feel you. I'm fresh out the joint, and I'm not trying to go back, and I damn sure don't want you and Islande going in. Aunt Medjine would cut my balls off and hand 'em to me," he joked.

Azon kept his thoughts to himself, but he doubted she'd cut Fabienne's nuts off. She'd gladly go for Azon's jugular for getting Islande caught up in some shit.

"I'm down, too," Islande agreed. "Three of us with three guns, I think we have a good chance. We just gotta catch them muhfuckas off guard. How we gon' get up in there?"

"I'm going to catch one of the employees when they're opening and put that chrome to their dome and follow her up in there with the two of you on my heels," Fabienne answered confidently. "As long as everyone cooperates, we won't have to let bullets spray in that bitch. I don't want to, but if push comes to shove, I'll eat a robbery charge. Not trying to catch no bodies."

Islande nodded his understanding because he agreed. Jail time wasn't ideal, but you never go into an illegal situation without weighing all of the possibilities, and jail was the most prevalent one of all. The men caught up and before they knew it, Fabienne was pulling up in the driveway of the small but nice house that Azon had rented. Azon had only spent his part of the money from Nice, on first month's rent, deposit, furniture, food, and household supplies. Initially, he was good with just an air mattress, but he decided that he wasn't going to be out there taking risks to be living like a pauper. He splurged on some nice, expensive furniture for him and his brother.

"I'm about to go to the crib. I'll be back to pick y'all up around seven PM. I've been casing the Internet Café since my second day home, and I know the second shift employees come in at seven and work until close at three AM."

"Bet." Azon nodded.

"This is nice, brother," Islande stated looking around the apartment. He leaned against the wall and eyed his ever-serious brother that always appeared to be in deep thought. "You ready to take Diamond Cove by storm?"

"That's the only reason I'm here," Azon stated more serious than he'd ever been about anything.

Islande grinned and extended his hand, so his brother could slap his palm. "My muhfuckin' nigga. Laplanche boys, baybeeeee."

Chapter four

The Internet Café heist had been a successful one with the men leaving the business with $84,000 in their possession. Fabienne knew that the Internet Café was owned by a husband and wife, but the wife wasn't present that night. In fact, the Café appeared to be short staffed which made the task of them robbing the place even easier for the men. Azon thought about the man that had robbed his parents' store. He knew firsthand that his parents were hardworking, humble people, and he didn't take too kindly to a man coming in and having the audacity to take what his parents worked for, and he had gone and done the same thing.

Azon didn't generally feel guilty about anything he did. Once the deed was done, he normally didn't ever think about it again. He refused to believe that he was getting soft, but something was nagging at him after the robbery. The $28,000 he made from the lick didn't even stop him from briefly thinking that maybe his mother was right. Maybe there wasn't any good in him. Or maybe, it was a hard knock life that turned him cold and numb. Azon knew he wasn't heartless because he'd go to war behind the people, he cared about but anybody else, fuck 'em, and it had always been that way.

Azon hadn't even been in Diamond Cove for two weeks, and he had already made $218,000. Fabienne had been on to something. Unless he had enough money to live off for three years or more, Azon would always feel that he didn't have enough money to be out here slacking, but tonight, he was going to hang out. He was taking a short break from plotting and planning his come-up. Fabienne made him aware that the racetrack on a Saturday night in Diamond Cove was where it was at. Azon could appreciate fast cars and motorcycles, so he was in there. The men went shopping earlier, and Azon bought an outfit that was nice, but it didn't cost more than $400 for the shoes, jeans, and shirt combined. He refused to spend most of what he had made so far on a bunch of designer shit. All that would come in due time. Besides when you were that nigga, you could fall up in an event in sweats and a plain tee and still be that nigga. Azon always knew it wasn't *on* him it was *in* him. He always ended up being the star of the show without even trying.

"It's thick as shit out here," Islande observed as they walked through the gates at the track.

"Told you," Fabienne responded. "Femmes sexy," he spoke in French which meant, sexy women as he ogled a thick, dark-skinned baddie.

The women were scantily clad and out in abundance. Islande licked his lips and rubbed his hands together like Birdman. He was from Florida, so Islande was used to seeing beautiful women, but these women were new to him and that made it all the more exciting.

"I've seen shorty three times since I've been in Diamond Cove," Azon stared at the beautiful woman with the box braids that he saw first at the gym and then at the fight. He watched her talk to the woman that she was with, and Azon couldn't help but to think that as corny as it might sound, it must be meant for him to know ole girl.

"Who?" Fabienne and Islande asked simultaneously.

"Baby in the black shorts and the box braids. Standing with the girl that has on the denim shorts."

It didn't take Islande or Fabienne long to spot the person that had Azon's attention to the point that he was damn near in a trance.

"Oh, she's nice for sure. Go get that," Islande urged.

"That's shorty from the gym and the fight? The one that fucks with Money?" Fabienne asked.

"Yeap. The one that was cheering for that whack ass nigga all loud at the boxing match that he barely won."

"Oh, she belongs to somebody?" Islande inquired as he watched a woman walk by. His eyes were glued to her ass so hard that he barely noticed that she had turned around as well to watch him as hard as he was watching her. When his eyes landed on her face, he smirked at the fact that she was eyeing him just as hard. The face was a smooth five, but the ass was a twenty. Because her face card wasn't valid, Islande didn't go after her. Being blessed with all that ass but hit in the face was crazy to him.

"What you gon' do?" Islande directed his attention back on Azon, who was still staring at shorty.

As if she felt three pairs of eyes on her, Gia looked over her shoulder, and when she locked eyes with Azon, her face flushed with embarrassment, and she quickly looked away.

"Oh, she'd fuck with you for sure," Islande noted.

Azon cocked his head slightly to the side. He wasn't so sure. She always acted so shy and demure anytime they exchanged glances. He could tell she was a good girl trying to be faithful to her nigga, and he applauded her effort. But how many times was he going to run into her without saying anything? He had tried on multiple occasions to respect her relationship, but the Universe kept throwing juicy lips in his face. Azon licked his lips as she walked over to the bleachers and appeared to be engrossed in the race that was about to start.

Azon walked over to her before he could talk himself out of it. He sat down beside the woman he kept running into and leaned in a little closer. "Who you think gon' win?" he asked. When she turned to face him, and her eyes widened, it made him chuckle, and her blush.

"Sorry to just be all in your space like this, but I've been in North Carolina for less than two weeks, and I've seen you three times. Either you're following me, or I'm supposed to at least have a conversation with you."

Gia smiled and shook her head. "Following you? Not hardly. But I do admit it's very weird that we keep running into each other. My name is Gia, and if I was a betting person, I'd say the guy on the all black bike is going to win."

Azon gave a slight head nod. "My name is Azon. It's nice to meet you, Gia. I take it you fuck with that lil' boxing cat. Money."

"Yes. That's my boyfriend."

Azon stroked his chin. "I can respect that, but if I run into you again, I'm gon' take that as a sign that I'm supposed to take you from that nigga."

Gia shifted nervously on the bleachers. He could tell by the reddening of her skin that he had her flushed. "I don't know about all of that. Maybe if you run into me again you just say hello and accuse me of following you."

"I can't make you any promises." Azon's eyes trailed the length of her body. "I might see you around sooner rather than later. I like to box a few times a week, and I see that we frequent the same gym."

Gia cleared her throat. "So it seems. I don't go a lot, but if I see you in there, I'll say hello."

"You do that. Have a nice night pretty girl."

"Thank you," Gia continued to blush as he got up and walked away.

"What's the word?" Islande asked as Azon walked back over to his brother and cousin.

"Nothing is the word. Calm down," Azon chuckled. "I just went over there to feel her out. Get her name and introduce myself. I'm trying to respect the fact that she has a man, but I told her if I run into her ass again, I'm taking her from that nigga."

"Straight like that," Fabienne agreed. "You got plenty of options until then, bro. The women been looking over here like they see something good to eat. You can probably try to crack on any woman out here and be able to bag that."

Azon's eyes scanned the crowd. There were some beautiful women in attendance but for whatever reason, none of them pulled him in like Gia did. Azon didn't know a thing about her, so he chalked it up to him being a man and wanting her because he knew he couldn't have her. It had been a little too long since he'd had sex and while he wasn't a pussy hound that had to be with a woman every night, a single woman on his team didn't sound like a bad idea. After a long, stressful day, it was always good to end the night balls deep inside a good smelling, soft woman. Azon eyed his prey for awhile before finally stopping a pretty brown-skinned female as she walked by. She was petite standing about 5'3 and only had a handful of ass, but he liked her locs that she wore up in a bun and the fact that she wasn't half-naked.

As he locked her number in his phone, something made Azon look up and when he did, he saw that Gia was watching him. When he caught her, she looked away hurriedly. Azon focused his attention back on the woman in front of him and promised her that he'd call. Something was telling him however, that he'd just be entertaining Ms. Fallon until the stars aligned, and he was able to get at Gia like he really wanted to.

***

Gia listened to Havanna talk a mile a minute, and it was hard for her to focus on anything that her friend was saying. It had been hours since she spoke to Azon at the racetrack, and the scent of his cologne still lingered in her nostrils. It took him being right up on her, inches away from her face for her to realize just how handsome he truly was. If Gia was a different kind of person, she would have used feeling neglected in her relationship as an excuse to do things with Azon that would get her a first-class ticket to hell on judgement day. Gia generally never grew tired of being a good person, but on this night, she wanted to allow him to do what he'd threatened. Hell, could he really take her from Money, if she was volunteering to go?

Gia wasn't sure what had come over her, but she didn't like it. To her knowledge, Money had never cheated on her and if she ever found out he had, she would just leave. Forget cheating back. She hated the way another man had invaded her thoughts. Since seeing him at the racetrack, Gia had thought about Azon more than she thought about her own man. She'd even missed his call while Azon was sitting next to her flirting with her, and she hadn't bothered to call him back. Why talk to Money when she could fantasize about Azon?

Since his latest win, he'd been doing exactly what she knew he would be doing. Celebrating with his friends and barely paying her any attention. Gia was over complaining about it because that changed absolutely nothing. Finally, Havanna was pulling up at Money's townhouse. She had been living there for a little over a year, and she still referred to the townhouse as Money's because it was. Havanna turned to look at her.

"I had fun with you tonight, boo. After tomorrow, I'll be back working like a Hebrew slave," she pushed out a dejected sigh.

Gia smiled. "I know, but think about how fat that bank account will be. I need to do some more marketing and promo for the boutique because it does well, but I need more. Enjoy that for sure money. Text me and let me know you made it home safely." Gia climbed out of her friend's jeep.

Money's car being in the driveway didn't mean he was home because most times he went out, he took an Uber or one of his friends drove. Money knew that getting a DUI would hurt his brand, so he rarely did it. When Gia entered the townhouse, however, she saw that he was indeed at home, listening to music, drinking cognac, and smoking his vape. He looked up at her.

"Why didn't you call me back? You were that busy doing whatever you were doing?" He appeared agitated, and Gia found that funny because he often did the same to her, and he hated when she bitched about it.

"You know it's loud at the racetrack. I didn't hear my phone, and by the time I realized I had a missed call, I was almost home anyway." She shrugged passively. "What did you want?"

Money eyed her for a bit as if he was trying to figure out if she was full of shit. "I know how Havanna can be sometimes. Don't get to following in behind her single ass and forget that you have a man at home. Especially when she's always in your ear telling you dumb shit."

Gia frowned and kissed her teeth because one thing she never did was throw her friends under the bus or tell him what they said. "You're always talking out your ass. First of all, I'm a grown woman. I don't follow in behind anybody, and second of all, Havanna don't be thinking about you. I stopped talking about my relationship a long time ago because I was tired of sounding like a broken record. We went to the racetrack then we went to the strip for less than an hour." Gia rolled her eyes and headed for the stairs.

It seemed that Money was content as long as she was at home, curled up on the couch, calling him. This one night, it was the other way around, and he was about to have a bitch fit. She was annoyed. Gia stomped up the stairs and into the master bathroom where she began to wash her face. She had just started the shower and began peeling off her clothes when she heard Money entering the bedroom. She was almost certain that he'd been drinking for hours, and he would probably be passed out by the time she finished cleaning her body and for once, she wouldn't be disappointed. As the washcloth slid over Gia's soapy breasts, her mind took her back to the infamous Azon, and her nipples hardened. Gia's clit swelled from the memory of him being so close to her, and she actually shivered.

What in the hell is wrong with me?

Gia's mind was blown that the mere thought of a man that she didn't know had relaxed the muscles in her face and taken her body to places that were usually reserved for her man. Azon was dangerous indeed, and Gia knew if she didn't begin to exercise some kind of self-control that she would allow him to get her into trouble. The person that usually played it safe had no desire for trouble. Or did she? Gia forced thoughts of Azon to the back of her mind, as she cleaned her body and turned the shower off. After drying off, she stood naked at the bathroom sink and brushed her teeth before putting a bonnet on over her braids and sauntering into the bedroom to put on a tank top and some panties, so she could get into bed. It hit Gia that she was exhausted as she stifled a yawn.

"Oh, I thought you'd be asleep." Gia was startled by Money who was sitting on the edge of their bed with red-rimmed eyes.

He didn't respond to her. His eyes roamed her body, and when his eyes landed back on her face, she could see the lust in his orbs. "Come sit on my face."

He didn't have to tell her twice and as Gia's agitation completely melted away, she got on the bed and mounted her man. Because of Money's vigorous pre-fight schedule off the top of her head, she couldn't even remember the last time they had sex. As Money's mouth locked around her pearl, Gia tossed her head back and licked her lips as she slowly rode her man's face. Her mouth fell into the shape of an *O,* and her breathing became labored as Money sucked and licked the most sacred parts of her body. He moaned into her treasure as her nectar became all his instead of hers. Gia's body shivered, and her stomach muscles contracted as he sucked her into a much needed release.

Gia peered down, but the only thing she could see was her man's eyes. The rest of his face was buried underneath her body. Gia cried out in ecstasy as her body jerked one last time, and then she wanted off Money's face because her pearl was super sensitive, and he was hungrily still licking and sucking. Reaching behind her, she massaged his hard tool through his basketball shorts and just as she suspected, he stopped sucking. Gia lifted herself off of him and turned around. Less than five seconds later, his manhood was in her mouth, and she was sucking feverishly. Money's dick wasn't super-sized, but it was the perfect fit for her, and Gia loved everything about it. She mostly only had orgasms if he performed oral sex on her, or if she stimulated her clit while they had sex, but she knew it had nothing to do with size. She'd only been with two guys before him, and neither of them could make her cum at all. Gia was in the percentage of women that rarely had orgasms from penetration alone, but she was cool with that. Her and Money still had tons of mind blowing sex, orgasm or no orgasm.

Money's moans turned her on as she deep throated him. He loved to hear her gag, and she loved to please him sexually. Something about a man moaning and praising her in the bedroom aroused her to the fullest.

"Ride this dick," Money groaned letting her know that he was ready to feel her.

Gia cleaned his tool up with her mouth and mounted him again but that time, she was sliding down on his erect member rather than gyrating on his face. They both moaned, and Gia stared down into the face of her lover. Good or bad, happy, or sad, he was hers, and she loved him. Money gripped her waist and closed his eyes as she rode him faster. She pressed her nub with her finger and gently began to rub in a circular motion as she rode Money. After only a few seconds, her moans were becoming louder as her belly contracted, and her vagina spasmed on his dick.

The tightening of her peach and the extra moistness that her orgasm brought made Money open his eyes and flip her over. He stared down into Gia's face as he drilled her middle. "I love you so much," she confessed before he erupted into her with a loud grunt.

Money took a moment to compose himself before rolling off of Gia. Not wanting to risk a UTI, she jumped up immediately to relieve her bladder and clean up making sure to bring a warm cloth back in the room to clean him off with. By the time Gia slid into the bed, Money was asleep and snoring with his mouth hanging open. All she could do was look at him and smile. The slight argument disappeared from her mind for the moment along with all of the feelings of neglect and abandonment. Gia laid down and pushed out a content sigh. For the first time in a few weeks, she went to sleep happy and hopeful that maybe the slight rough patch that her relationship seemed to be hitting was coming to an end.

Five

Azon had just stepped out of the house to head to the grocery store when his phone vibrated in his pocket. He ate fast food on occasion, especially when he was busy, but not too much. Growing up with the parents that he had, fast food was a luxury that they were only afforded maybe once a month. Medjine and Michael saw no need to waste money on takeout when they had food at home, and it often tasted way better than the food in the restaurants. Both his mother and father could burn in the kitchen, and they made sure all of their kids could cook too. Johanne had cooked quite a few meals for Azon and Islande since their arrival in Diamond Cove, but they'd still been eating out more than they were used to, and Azon's stomach was fucked up. He planned to fill the kitchen and cook for his damn self.

When Azon slid his phone from his pocket, he saw that Fabienne was calling, and he didn't hesitate to answer. Azon hit the unlock button on the key fob for his brand-new Camaro that Jeanne put in her name for him. When a person is out in the streets engaging in illegal activities, they never want to put expensive items, or anything in their name for that matter. He wanted to stay as low under the radar as possible. Azon gave Jeanne $9,000 to put down on the $60,000 car. He also gave her $2,000 for her pocket, and he planned to double up on the car payments for the first year before finally paying it off. Azon knew he had to move smart when it came to large amounts of money because he didn't want the IRS to be notified.

"Sak Pase?" Azon cradled the phone between his ear and shoulder as he got into the car. The new car smell wafting off the leather seats infiltrated his nostrils.

"N'ap Boule," Fabienne replied before kissing his teeth. "Yo, I need you to come get me from this bitch's spot. Like ASAP my nigga before I go to jail. I had to take the rental car back that my mom's got me and against my better judgement, I let Khloe get me a car, now she won't let me leave with it. If she calls the police, I just might put hands on her, so get me away from here. Please."

Azon could hear the urgency in his cousin's tone, and he knew the man wanted to avoid jail. When some people walk away easily and are quiet and reserved, it can give off the wrong impression that the person is soft, but Azon knew all too well the kind of hell that Fabienne could raise when he was set off. The pleading in his tone was the calm before the storm. Azon could hear a woman yelling in the background, and he knew that Khloe and Fabienne must have been into it. He also knew that if he didn't get his people away from there quick, he might end up regretting it.

"I'm on the way. Already in the car. Text me the address."

"Thank you, brother."

Fabienne and Azon were cousins, but 'brother' was a term of endearment reserved for those that were truly like a brother to the men. When Azon put the address in his GPS, he saw that he was thirteen minutes away from where Fabienne was. He didn't have anything illegal in the car, so he broke the speed limit trying to get there in a time faster than what the app predicted. When Azon pulled up, Fabienne was standing in the yard leaning against a rental car with a deep scowl embedded on his face. A very attractive woman was all in his face yelling in an animated fashion with her hands going every which way. There were very few domestic violence disputes that Azon would involve himself in, but for Fabienne, he knew he needed to get him away from this woman before he left the scene in cuffs.

When Fabienne saw Azon pulling up in the driveway, he attempted to walk around Khloe, but she jumped in front of him and placed her entire palm over his face. She pushed his head back hard and fast, and Fabienne grabbed her by the neck and shook her quickly before letting her neck go.

"I swear to God on my mama, if you don't leave me the fuck alone, I will act like the nigga you're trying to get me to be. You already scratched my face," Fabienne growled. "If you touch me again, I'm knocking you the fuck out."

Khloe's adrenaline wouldn't allow her to back down, and she hopped right back in Fabienne's face. "You're not leaving! You're going to talk to me like a man!"

Fabienne stepped around Khloe and locked eyes with Azon who had gotten out of the car. "Brother, please, tell this broad what the fuck is good for her." He was once again begging, and Azon knew he was at his wits' end. A fresh scratch on his cheek and the darkness in his eyes made Azon aware that his cousin was a ticking time bomb. Azon didn't know Khloe from a can of paint, but he stepped into her line of vision and tried to reason with her.

"Shorty, I don't know you, but if Fabienne is trying to walk away, I need you to let him. I don't need him in handcuffs looking like the bad guy because you're over here provoking him. If he's trying to walk away, let him," he repeated with finality. "Once he's no longer upset, then maybe he'll talk to you."

Khloe wanted to pop off on the sexy stranger that was standing in her face, but something in his eyes told her to leave well enough alone. She didn't fear Fabienne as she should because he loved her, or at least she hoped he did. But there was a nagging voice that kept telling her she shouldn't keep pushing her luck because something in this man's eyes swayed her to believe that he wasn't wrapped too tight. Laughter roared from behind Azon, and he turned to see what was so funny.

Fabienne was genuinely laughing. A complete contrast to the emotion that he'd just displayed. "Yooo," Fabienne placed a hand on his belly that was aching from his boisterous laughter. "This slut fucked my man, Sabien while I was locked up. Like my partner since high school. The only nigga that really kept money on my books for real when I was away. The same nigga that was there with me when I caught my charge for fucking up Taj. This slut," he pointed at Khloe, and the grin was instantly wiped from his face, and the darkness was back in his orbs. "She had sex with the nigga in the same bed that my dumb ass laid in when I came home. I will never talk to this whore again." He folded his tall body to get inside of Azon's car, and Azon turned to eye Khloe.

With a sheepish expression on her face, she swallowed hard and tried to mask the shame that she felt, but Azon could see the guilt written all over her face. There was no need for him to say anything else. He turned and walked towards the car. Once he was inside, Khloe turned to trek back inside of her home feeling defeated. Since the car had never been turned off, Azon placed the gear in reverse and looked over at Fabienne.

"You good?"

Fabienne released a low, angry chuckle. "If I'm not good, it'll never be because of a disloyal hoe. I tried to come home and make it work because I thought she held me down while I was gone, and I felt I owed her that much. My feelings aren't hurt that she's not as solid as I thought, and now I have to go chase new pussy. She did me a favor for real. That muhfucka isn't the one for me. I was with her more so out of obligation. And Sabien, he just did what fuck niggas do. That's why when it comes to getting money and certain shit, I only fuck with you and Islande. I'll never fully trust an outsider, and this is why."

Azon nodded his understanding. "You want me to take you to your mom's house? I was just about to go to the grocery store. I'm not meeting with ole' boy until later."

Fabienne had turned Azon on to a heroin plug that he trusted and was convinced was good people. When it came to Fabienne, Azon, and Islande, they all wanted to be heavy hitters. They weren't setting out with the goal of making small money. There was only so much working their way up they were willing to do, so Fabienne was going to deal with coke. Azon was going to sell heroin, and Islande was going to sell weed. Islande actually had his own weed connect back in Florida, and he was going to get two females to transport the pounds that he planned to buy to Diamond Cove. Each man had a lane, and they planned to stay in theirs.

"Yeah. I'm just going to go ahead and see if she can go get the loan from the bank today to get me a car. I've been trying to wait, so I can come up with a legit justification for why I have the money to be able to afford a car payment. I told her last week that I got my old welding job back. She's still going to be suspicious if I get a car and a place this fast, so I guess I'll stay at her crib for a few more weeks. I'm just not up for the lectures. She swears if I go back to prison, she's done with me."

Azon chuckled. "Don't even get your boxer briefs in a bunch behind that one. You know that's a lie."

Fabienne laughed because he knew it too. "We're far from broke, and we're about to have a for sure way to bring some money in, so I say we enjoy ourselves a few more nights before we get into grind mode. Let's hit a sports bar or something tonight."

Azon kissed his teeth. "Nigga, you're trying to enjoy your way into some new pussy."

"That too. Shit, why should I have to wait? If I'm free, then I'm free."

"I feel you. We can do that. I might hit that Fallon chick up later on and see what she's up to. I'm starting to feel like I'm in prison being around you and Islande all day. I need some company that consists of ass and titties."

The men conversed until Azon arrived at Johanne's house, and Fabienne got out of the car. For the most part, Azon had tunnel vision. His goals consisted of getting money and not much else. As long as he wasn't walking around broke, then all was well in his life, but he was twenty-five. Maybe it was time to have some other goals outside of money. But what, a wife and some kids? Azon chuckled inwardly because he didn't see that happening anytime soon but lowkey, he wanted a love like his parents shared. Together for almost twenty-seven years, and he could count on one hand how many times he'd seen them argue. Love like that was rare, however, and Azon would be damned if he gave his all to a woman like Khloe. So until the stars aligned in his favor, he'd be a single man doing what single men did.

***

Hours later, Azon had checked grocery shopping off of his to do list and had cooked up an amazing meal that him and Islande demolished. He had also met with the plug and secured enough heroin to make him a very nice profit once it was all sold. Things were looking up for Azon, and he didn't have a thing to complain about. Two weeks in a new city, and he had a car, a place to live, and a fat stash. Sure, he had to get it by ungodly means, but it was what it was. Since things were going the way he needed them to go, Azon didn't see anything wrong with splurging on a nice outfit for the evening. He had been eyeing a diamond encrusted chain, but that purchase would have to wait. He wasn't trying to do too much too fast. The car and house were secured, so diamonds could wait, but an outfit was feasible.

Azon was parked outside of a shoe store when *she* caught his eye. "Got damn what is it with this chick?" Azon mumbled to himself. He had seen Gia too many times for it not to be some kind of sign. He had been joking when he told her if he saw her again, he was taking her from her nigga but obviously, the Universe was trying to call his bluff.

Azon watched her disappear inside a boutique, and he got out of his car and headed in the same direction. A bell chimed above the door alerting his entrance. Azon looked around the store, and he only saw women's clothes, shoes, and accessories until an open space behind the register made him aware that there was a side for men as well. His eyes danced around the room until his gaze landed on her. Behind the register. The woman standing next to her was talking to her, but Gia's orbs were trained on Azon. With a smirk on his face, he walked towards the register and waited for the conversation to end.

"Hi. Can I help you?" Gia asked. She made an attempt to sound professional, but he could tell she was shook. She looked almost afraid of what these very frequent encounters meant.

"I told you what was gon' happen the next time I saw you, so how you gon' break it to that nigga that you can't be with him anymore?"

Gia chuckled while his expression remained serious. Her employee's brows lifted as she eased away from the obvious flirting that was taking place. The man in Gia's face was too fine, and she was slightly envious. Gia already had a fine man meanwhile, she was single as hell.

"How can I help you, sir?" Gia repeated ignoring his brazen statement.

"I just came in here to find an outfit for tonight. Nothing too fancy because I'm just going to a sports bar." Azon felt the need to fall back a tad, so she would be comfortable in his presence. He didn't want to overwhelm her or come off like a weirdo. It would be too easy to believe that he was stalking her versus believing that they kept having these chance encounters. Diamond Cove was way too big of a city for that.

"I didn't know you worked here." He added, and Gia smiled.

"Work here, I guess I kind of do, but I own the place."

Azon gave an appreciative nod. "That's what's up. I guess I have to show out then and blow a lil' bag," he winked at her. "Show me your best stuff."

"Right this way." Gia led him to the men's side. She didn't know enough about him to really know what his taste was, but she was going to suggest items that she liked to see her man in. 'Urban' dressing was cool especially for laid back days, but Gia liked to see her man in something besides jeans and tees.

She spent a lot of time on social media looking at trends, then coming in her boutique and putting together items that would look good together. Her mannequins stayed fly. Gia got lost in pulling pieces for Azon to try on and while she was doing that, he was ogling her. Gia was dressed in camo print cargo shorts with a fitted, beige, belly shirt. On her feet were nude flip flops with a bow on the toe, and the bow was decorated in spikes. The baggy shorts and the tight shirt gave her a super sexy vibe, and her long braids were piled on top of her head in a bun. Her nails and toes both had French tips, and she smelled like peaches. The two Cuban link ankle bracelets made her appearance even sexier, and Azon's mouth was watering for a taste of her. Fuck being respectful of her relationship.

Temptation was being waved in his face crazy, and Azon was ready to dance with the devil.

Gia turned around and shoved an armful of items in his hands. "The dressing room is right that way," she jerked her head in the direction of the fitting room.

"Nah, I don't have to try them on," Azon's eyes drifted downward towards the items she'd given him. "I trust your taste. As long as they're my size, I'm good."

"Okay," she replied and led him to the register, so he could look through the sizes.

Gia didn't want to stare at him while he sorted through the clothes, but she couldn't take her eyes off of him. Why did she keep seeing this fine ass man? In the entire two years that she'd been with Money, she'd never been tempted like this. Not even when a super fine social media influencer saw her in the club one night and was on her like white on rice. He was fine with a body to die for but one conversation with him, and Gia could see that he was an arrogant, self-centered asshole, and she didn't care how fine he was. He had the personality of a beaver. When she came into contact with men like that, it was super easy to brush them off and appreciate what she had at home, but Azon was giving her different signals. Gia hated that she was even curious about what he had going on. He said he was new in town and with the way he flirted with her, she would hope he was single, but these days, you never know.

"Everything looks good." Azon smiled when he raised his head and caught her staring.

Gia cleared her throat and began ringing the items up. Her body was still warm from embarrassment, when he spoke.

"When you gon' let me take you out?"

Gia shook head before looking up at him. "I know you know I have a man, so I'm not even sure if you really expect an answer from me."

"God don't want you with that nigga."

The seriousness in his tone made Gia laugh. "What?"

"I told you. We keep running into each other for a reason. I don't know what that reason is. The only thing I can guess is that you're supposed to be with me."

Gia pushed out a deep sigh. She would never in a million years admit to him that she damn near agreed. Or maybe God was just testing her. She was on Money to fight for their relationship, and if she could be so easily moved by a stranger, maybe she didn't deserve the kind of man that she wanted Money to be. Only time would tell if he would get his shit together, but Gia knew she had to play her part too. She couldn't let being unhappy sometimes be the reason that she cheated on her partner. She despised it when men found excuses to cheat, and she never wanted to include herself in the games and the fuckery. She offered Azon a small smile.

"That sounds really nice and romantic, but my man wouldn't appreciate that.

Azon simply nodded because while he felt that he kept running into her for a reason, he couldn't ever be mad at her wanting to be faithful to her nigga. That just meant that when he finally did get her, he'd be able to trust her.

"That will be $477," Gia stated when she was done ringing the merchandise up.

Azon pulled a wad of money from his pocket and counted out $500. "Keep the change."

Gia counted the money as her eyes darted from the bills in her hand to his face. "Are you sure?"

"Positive. I love to see a black woman doing her thing." He winked at her, grabbed his bag, and left leaving Gia stuck staring after him.

"Girl, who is that?" Ajonique, Gia's employee flew over to her as soon as Azon left the store.

"A guy that I keep running into."

"Well, he needs to run into me. You're taken, and you clearly don't want him. I'd ride that D until my legs lock up." Ajonique stared at the door lustfully, and Gia hated the surge of jealousy that shot through her.

It wouldn't matter who he ended up with. It couldn't be her. Gia tried to convince herself that she wasn't into Azon like that, but a blind man could see that he had her in a chokehold.

"Next time he comes in shoot your shot," she said to Ajonique not really meaning what she was saying.

"I damn sure will 'cus that man is too fine!"

Six

Gia stood in the doorway of her bedroom with a mean pout on her face and tears in her eyes as she watched Money pack his suitcase. He hadn't said anything else about London so foolishly, she made reservations at a popular restaurant for his birthday only to come home two days before to find him packing.

"You're really going to London?" she asked as her bottom lip quivered.

Money looked over his shoulder at her. "Yeah. My flight leaves in the morning at seven. You don't have to take me to the airport because I know that's early."

Gia narrowed her eyes and jerked her head back. "I don't have to take you to the airport? Money, you got me fucked up. We didn't do anything together on Valentine's Day and now you're spending your birthday with your friends. If you want to be single, just say that."

Money threw his hands in the air in an exasperated manner. "Here we fucking go. I'm not gon' argue about this shit with you. The flight is booked. I'll be in London for five days. It is what it is," he shrugged passively as if her feelings truly didn't matter.

Gia stared at his back for a few moments before turning to walk away. Angrily, she brushed the tears away that were streaming down her cheeks and vowed that would be the last time that she ever cried over Money. If he didn't care about their relationship, then she didn't care either. He didn't have to spend every waking moment with her, but Gia knew she wasn't wrong for wanting her man to show her some attention.

When he was preparing for a fight, she left him alone. She dealt with his vigorous schedule and accommodated his every need. He could ask her to drive five hours away to get him a special kind of bottled water, and she'd do it because that's what you did in relationships. Clearly, they weren't on the same page, and she was tired of feeling like she was begging him to see her. If he would rather put everything else before her, she had no choice but to accept it.

Gia sat on the couch and pulled her knees up to her chest. She just had to figure out what her next move was. She lived in his home and at her big age, moving back in with her parents wasn't an option that she wanted to entertain. She had $7,000 saved and while that was enough to move, she feared that if the boutique didn't start bringing in more money that she'd be struggling. She had to do what she had to do though and to convince herself that she was serious, Gia went online and began looking at one bedroom apartments. She found some nice ones for under $1,500 a month, and she requested to do a tour for two of them the following day. Gia really couldn't believe that she was looking for her own apartment, but things had gotten just that bad. Trying to reason with Money was too much like beating a dead horse, and she was truly exhausted. Maybe they just needed space. Maybe an apartment was too much. Maybe she could get a hotel room for a week or two, and that would be the thing to make him come to his senses.

An hour had gone by, and he still hadn't come downstairs to check on her. The more reality set in that Money just didn't care for her the way she cared for him, it hurt. It hurt real bad, and that would be one of the hardest parts about leaving. The misery. The heartbreak, and the lonely nights crying herself to sleep. But she reasoned with herself, there were lonely nights that she cried herself to sleep while in a relationship with him, so what would the difference really be?

Gia didn't even have the desire to sleep in the bed next to him. She doubted sleep would come anyway. She thought about the custom sneakers she ordered him for his birthday that ran her $300. They were going back to the store expeditiously. If Money didn't do anything else, he spent money on her, but she didn't feel petty for wanting to return the shoes because most of the things he bought her, he did it on his own. Gia never asked him for anything. There would be random cash apps for $3,000 with a note attached saying *get inventory for boutique*. There were times he came to her boutique and spent $1,000 on clothes, wore them, tagged her in social media posts, and her online orders would start going crazy. People loved seeing one of their favorites in something that they could easily afford to stunt in. It was easier for a lot of his followers to buy the items that Money had from her boutique that would run them $100 for an outfit versus them trying to buy the Gucci, Balenciaga, and Fendi that he wore.

Money paid all the bills, and he often paid for her self-care. At the beginning of every month, Gia spent two full days on self-care. Hair, lashes, nails, pedicure, facials, chemical peels, laser hair removal, massages, candle hauls, and buying cute pajama sets and underwear was her guilty pleasure. Her self-care could run up to $1,500 maybe more. She never had to think twice about the price or the tip because she often paid for the services with his Amex card. He spoiled her with material items, and most people felt that should have been enough. They would look at her like she was the problem because she'd rather spend holidays and birthdays with him, and she craved his time. Gia would have been just as happy laid up on the couch watching movies and eating snacks with Money as she would be if he bought her a purse. It wasn't rocket science at all, but he simply didn't get it.

Despite the fact that she promised herself she wouldn't cry anymore, a tear made its' way out of the corner of her eye and dripped onto the throw pillow that she'd placed her head on. They had been together for two years. Mourning the end of the relationship would be inevitable and as much as she didn't want to, Gia knew she was going to have to allow herself to feel all of the emotions. She couldn't skip through them and ignore them. She had to sit with them, process them, and let them pass. That would be the excruciatingly hard part.

Sleep finally found her in the wee hours of the morning, and it seemed as if as soon as she closed her eyes, she heard Money in the kitchen. Gia's eyes fluttered open, and she saw that the time was 5 AM. She swallowed hard as her stiff body reminded her that she'd slept on the couch and though it was expensive and made of the best leather, she didn't feel good after laying on it for hours. The dull ache in her heart reminded her of why she'd slept on the couch, and Gia didn't want to face the day let alone Money. She closed her eyes and with a racing heart pretended to be asleep. The moment of clarity would be if he woke her up to say goodbye, or if he walked out of the door without waking her or kissing her.

The alarm system notified her that the front door was open, and Gia held her breath. When the door closed gently behind Money, a gut-wrenching sob pushed from her throat. It was over. It was painfully and undeniably over.

***

Gia knew the boutique wouldn't see her for a day maybe even two. The last time she missed days at the boutique, it was a few years back when she had covid. After Money left, Gia dragged herself up the stairs and got into the bed that he left unmade. On one hand she was heartbroken and on the other hand, she hated his guts. Someone as selfish as him didn't deserve her tears. Gia curled up into a fetal position and slept until ten AM. When she finally got up, it was only because she needed to relieve her bladder. She had the house to herself for five days, but Gia knew she needed to start the process of getting her own place. It would be great if she could be gone by the time he came back. If she could have it her way, Gia would spend the rest of the day in bed sulking, but she had two apartments that she needed to go view. As she brushed her teeth and stared at her pitiful reflection in the mirror, an idea popped into her head.

No.

Gia knew it was a bad idea, and she tried to push the thought from her head, but it was no use. As soon as she stepped into her closet to find something to wear, temptation was pulling at her again. "If it's meant for me to see him I will. If not, I will at least get a workout in," she mumbled to herself.

After much contemplation, Gia finally threw on some peach-colored leggings with a matching sports bra, and she stuffed her feet into her white gym shoes. She was going to the gym and if Azon was there, she'd know that the Universe really was on some other shit. She hadn't even officially left Money yet, and Gia knew she was playing a dangerous game, but so what? Why couldn't she feel good for once? Gia pulled her hair back into a ponytail and used a spoolie to fluff her lashes before spraying on some perfume. She hated when she was sad or pissed off because her appetite would be nonexistent and though she felt she could stand to lose a few pounds, that's not the way she wanted to lose weight. Letting a fuck nigga take her appetite was the definition of going out sad, but Gia knew fixing herself some breakfast would be a waste of time.

She had no idea how often Azon went to the gym, if he had a set time that he went, or if he would even show that day, but she was trying her luck. In her heart of hearts, she knew she didn't need to see him, but that didn't stop the desire from being there. Had she been looking for a reason? Gia had to wonder if she was overreacting because she wanted to see Azon, flirt with him, and entertain him without feeling guilty.

"Nope, you will not do that to yourself," she chastised herself. "You are not crazy. You have every reason to be upset. Don't let that nigga or anyone else make you think you're tripping." Gia didn't care if she was talking to herself. She was saying some real shit. Shit that she needed to hear.

Gia finally pulled up at the gym, and another self-induced peptalk was necessary. She had to convince herself that working out would do her body good, and whether she ran into Azon or not, the trip wouldn't be wasted. She had come to the gym without Money plenty of times before but for whatever reason, this time felt awkward. Gia knew that once she moved out of the townhouse, and the relationship was officially done that she'd have to find a new gym. This was Money's stomping grounds, and she refused to risk running into him once they were done. Gia had no desire to do the break-up to make-up song and dance. She initially thought that maybe they needed a break but no. They were adults. A break shouldn't be necessary for him to get his act together.

As she walked into the gym, Gia wondered if she was stupid. A woman like Havanna would have bought a ticket to London, first class, and popped up on her man invited or not. She would have inserted herself into the trip and got down to the bottom of whether it was actually a guy's trip or if Money was with another woman. Just the thought made Gia's breath hitch in her throat. Maybe he was cheating. That might be the better explanation because if he'd truly rather take such an interesting and once in a lifetime trip with his friends rather than her something was really wrong.

Gia pushed all of her negative thoughts to the back of her mind, turned on her Beats headphones, and got on the Stairmaster. The City Girls provided just the motivation that she needed to push through this workout.

'If you look good, act bad. If you look good, act bad.'

Gia repeated the anthem over and over in her head and when the song was done, she played it again. When the song finished for the second time, she went straight to Glorilla's hit, *Tomorrow*.

"When I lose a nigga, I just pop and go find some mo'," Gia rapped underneath her breath while trying to control her breathing.

Before she knew it, thirty minutes had passed on the Stairmaster, and sweat was dripping down her neck. Gia's eyes darted around the room, so she could figure out what she wanted to do next. Just as she decided on doing leg presses, it happened. *He* came into the gym with two other guys, and Gia almost tripped. This man was either her soulmate or the devil, but he didn't keep showing up in her life for no reason.

Gia had managed to look away before he could catch her ogling him, but after a minute or so, she felt someone's gaze burning a hole through her, and she was willing to bet that it was him. She didn't look though. After forty minutes on the machine, Gia stopped it and chugged a half a bottle of water while she tried to catch her breath. As soon as she stepped off the Stairmaster, she almost ran into him.

His lips moved, but she couldn't hear what he said, so she tapped her phone screen to pause the music that was playing loudly in her ear. "Say what?"

"I said what colors?"

Confusion made Gia's eyes narrow. She had no clue what he was talking about. "Colors? What do you mean what colors?"

"For our wedding?"

A genuine smile stretched across her face as she tried to imagine his sexy ass being her husband. "You're crazy," she shook her head bashfully.

Before he could respond, a pain ripped through her right side that was so intense, that Gia's eyes bulged out of her head, and she took a step back, so she could lean over the machine. When Azon saw the pained look on her face and the way that she was gripping her side, he became concerned.

"Yo you good?" He was supposed to be sparring with Fabienne, but he couldn't not come speak to her.

Gia took a deep breath and prayed that the pain would subside. She hoped it was just an exercise cramp or something that would pass but after a full minute, the searing pain shooting through her side was enough to make her knees buckle. Sweat decorated her forehead, and her chest heaved up and down. Gia had never felt pain so intense in her life. This didn't come from overexerting herself in the gym. This was something else.

"My side. It hurts really really bad." She couldn't even look Azon in the eyes as she spoke. The pain had her on the verge of tears, and Azon could tell by the distressed look on her face that she was not okay.

"Where's your car? I'm about to drive you to the hospital." Gia's entire face was red, and she was gritting her teeth together. She didn't look good at all.

With the amount of pain that Gia was in, she would have agreed to let Azon carry her piggyback to hell if it would end the torture that she was enduring. Gia took slow, steady breaths in an effort to keep herself calm. She was on the verge of tears, and the hospital sounded like a wonderful idea. It didn't matter that she didn't know Azon. She retrieved her keys and passed them to him. Before she could take a step, Azon had swooped her up in his arms bridal style and was whisking her off towards the door. The relief she felt from not having to walk made Gia's body somewhat relax in Azon's arms.

Patrons of the gym were looking to see what was going on. Especially Fabienne and Islande. Islande approached his brother and asked him what was going on. "Que se passe-t-il?"

"Elle souffre." Azon let his brother know that Gia was in pain. He would let Islande figure out the rest.

"The red Kia parked right over here near the front," Gia told Azon as he walked out of the gym carrying her as easily as if she weighed nothing.

Azon located her vehicle, unlocked the doors, and gently eased her inside.

"Do you have a hospital that you prefer?" he looked over at her as he started the car.

"Diamond Cove Memorial is closest. It's like six minutes away." Gia laid her head back on the seat and closed her eyes while still gripping her side. She'd had days in the gym where she pushed herself until she felt like she would throw up, and she'd never felt pain like this. It was damn near like she'd ripped something.

Azon hurriedly typed the destination into the GPS on his phone and followed the directions to get Gia to the hospital. He weaved in and out of traffic with the skill of a race car driver. Azon was breaking the speed limit and damn near running red lights, and Gia didn't even care. She appreciated the fact that he really didn't know her from a can of paint, and he'd abandoned his plans and his friends without a second thought to get her some help. She would never forget that. The car ride was silent aside from the soft sounds of Bryson Tiller wafting through the vehicle's speakers. Every minute or so, Azon would glance over at Gia, and her eyes would still be closed.

When he arrived at the hospital, Azon drove up to the emergency room drop off and hopped out of the car. Opening her door, he once again cradled her in his arms and carried her inside to look for a wheelchair. A nurse saw him coming in and rushed a wheelchair over towards him.

"What's going on today?" the nurse asked.

"My right side. It hurts really bad." Gia's eyes had tears in them. Fighting the pain had become almost unbearable for her.

When the nurse began to push her towards the back, Azon went to find a parking space, and then he went right back inside. Fifteen minutes later, it was confirmed that Gia's appendix had ruptured, and she needed emergency surgery. The nurse informed Azon that surgery would take about an hour and since Gia hadn't had the chance to call anyone to come be with her, Azon decided to stay with her. He sat in the waiting room texting Islande and Fabienne and avoiding phone calls from his customers. He wouldn't be able to move for the next few hours, so they'd have to get heroin from someone else. Azon hated to miss money, but Gia was more important. Someone that he barely knew but obviously wanted to get to know. Once she got out of surgery she might give him the boot and call her man to come up there, and that would be fine too. Azon was polite, and he was a gentleman, but he wasn't pressed. Well, when it came to Gia he wasn't *that* pressed. She definitely had his attention, however.

His mouth was a little dry, so Azon ventured to the cafeteria to get something to snack on and a drink. An hour and a half later, the nurse was coming to get him, and he followed her to the back. Gia was just waking up and still appeared groggy and a bit confused.

"Do you want something to drink?" the nurse asked Gia as she typed something into the computer. "We have Sprite, Ginger ale, apple juice, cranberry juice, and orange juice."

"Ginger ale," Gia replied in a raspy voice then looked over at Azon. Her brows furrowed as if she didn't expect him to be there.

Azon walked over to the chair that was placed beside the bed and sat down. "You good?" he asked her.

Gia closed her eyes and breathed in deeply through her nose. "Yes. Finally. I have never felt pain like that. I thought I was dying. Thank you for bringing me here. I didn't think you'd stay though."

"Why would you think that?" His tone was gentle and serious and fresh out of surgery, high off pain medication, and groggy off anesthesia, he still managed to turn Gia on. She'd never seen anything like it in her life. His accent, his subtle flirting, and the way he handled her with care were only adding to his long list of good attributes.

"I don't know. Because you don't know me, and I know you probably have things to do."

"Nothing more important than making sure you were good. Do you have anybody you want me to call for you? You want me to call your corny ass nigga?"

Just the mention of Money made Gia sad, but she still chuckled. Azon really didn't like the fact that she had a man, but she thought that was cute. She swallowed the lump in her throat. "He's in London with his friends, and I'm pretty sure we broke up." It was the first time she'd said it out loud.

Azon didn't even try to pretend to be sad for her. The smirk on his face told her all she needed to know, and Gia shook her head and smiled bashfully. "Too soon, Azon."

He threw his hands up in surrender. "I didn't even do anything. I won't be fake and say some shit like I'm sorry. So, I just won't say shit." All he needed was a chance. Azon was smart enough to know that sometimes, break-ups were only temporary. But he felt with free reign to apply pressure, if she ended up going back to Money after that, then they just weren't meant to be. It was as simple as that.

He knew her heart might need time to heal, but he wasn't trying to propose to her. Azon simply wanted to be in her space.

"Understandable," she responded. "If you can pass me my phone, I'll call my parents. I'm sure they'll rush right up here, and you'll be free to go. Thank you once again for bringing me."

"No thanks necessary. I did what a decent person would." He passed Gia her phone and listened as she called her mother then her father. When it was confirmed that they were on the way, he stood up.

"Take my number and call me if you need anything."

Gia unlocked her phone and put Azon's number in.

"On second thought," he took the phone from her small hand and called the number that she'd just stored. Azon called himself from her phone. "I need to have your number too, because something tells me you'll be on that good bullshit."

Gia giggled and waited for him to give her, her phone back. When he was done, his serious eyes bore into hers. "Get some rest. Call me if you need me," he repeated, and Gia's stomach caved in.

There were a lot of things she might possibly need him for and most of them made her ashamed to think about so soon after her break-up. "I will," she promised softly. Gia bit her bottom lip as she watched his gap legged walk out of the room. That man, that man, that man. He was something real damn serious.

Seven

Two days later, Gia was at her parents' house irritated beyond belief. She was still slightly sore, and she had just broken the news to her father that her and Money had broken up. Her parents suggested that she come to their house when she left the hospital because they knew Money was out of town, and they wanted to take care of her. Blake had just come into Gia's old bedroom and mentioned that if she wanted, he would drop her off at home the day Money was supposed to come back, which was in two days. She broke the news that she wasn't going back, and she watched her father's face crumple with confusion.

"What do you mean you aren't going back?"

This was a conversation that she'd wanted to avoid for a little bit longer. Thanks to her pain medication, Gia had been doing a lot of sleeping and when her parents weren't in the room talking to her, her sister was over visiting. Being around her family had done wonders for her spirit. Azon had even been texting her and checking on her, and that made her smile. The one person that hadn't called and checked on her was Money. He hit her with one sorry ass *good morning, babe,* text message his second day in London, and Gia didn't even respond. She had a dream the night before that he was in London with another woman, and she woke up in tears. Gia knew she had a long road ahead of getting Money out of her heart and her head.

"I broke up with Money, daddy. I want my own place. I was supposed to go look at apartments the day my appendix ruptured. I'm going to have to put that off until I can drive again, but I'm not going back to his house unless it's to get my things."

"What happened?" Blake asked curiously.

"A lot of things, daddy. It wasn't just one thing, but him going to London without me when he knew I wanted to go was the last straw. I just think we've run our course."

Blake stared at his daughter for a few seconds, and Gia knew him well enough to know that when he didn't agree with her right away, he was about to say some shit that she wouldn't like.

"He has a fight coming up in five weeks. This isn't what he needs right now. Does he know about the break-up? Is he upset?"

Gia's jaw slacked. She was seriously appalled. She drew back and furrowed her brows. "Really daddy? That's all you care about? I don't think he knows about the break-up and from the way he acts, I'm sure he doesn't care. I, however, am a little sad, but I'll be fine thanks for asking," she finished dryly.

Blake shrugged unapologetically. "How many times did I tell you not to deal with that nigga? You just had to have him. Everything I told you went out of the window, and you defied me in every way to be with him. You got what you wanted and that's fine, but that doesn't change the fact that Money and I have business together. I don't care about that personal shit because I told both of you that at this point in his career, he didn't need to be in a relationship. Y'all let hormones lead the way, and I'm letting my brain lead mine. I don't want him losing that fight because he's off his game."

Gia had never cursed in front of her parents, and she didn't want to start that day. Out of respect for her father, she eased out of bed wincing slightly. She no longer wanted to be in his home.

"What you about to do? Leave? You in your feelings, so you gon' walk around pouting not speaking to me?" Blake knew his daughter all too well.

With a scowl on her face, she ignored her father, grabbed some clothes from the bag of personal items her sister had brought her, and went into the bathroom to get dressed. She would text Havanna, and hopefully her friend was home. If not, she'd check into a hotel. Since Money wasn't home, she'd even go back to his house for a night or two, but she was leaving her parents' house ASAP. Maybe she had brought all of this on herself for being a helpless romantic. Maybe she should have listened to her father, but she hadn't, and the damage was done. He acted like it would kill him to give her just a little empathy. Let that tough love bullshit go for just one second and just be a loving father. That seemed like too much to ask of him. Gia was angry, and tears stung her eyes. She just wanted to crawl into a hole and be away from everyone and everything.

The act of moving around and getting dressed made her uncomfortable, but Gia kept moving as if she didn't feel a thing. She may have been being a brat, but she didn't care. Her father had actually looked her in the face and basically told her that he hoped the break-up didn't negatively impact Money's upcoming fight. To hell with her because her grown ass had dared go against his wishes and date someone that she had actually fallen in love with. When Gia emerged from the bathroom, her father was no longer in the room.

Gia made the bed, grabbed her bag, and left the room. As soon as her foot hit the bottom step, her mother rounded the corner. When they locked eyes, Gia could see the apologetic undertone in her mother's eyes.

"Gia, where are you going? You aren't all the way healed. You know how your father is. You have to ignore him sometimes. He's bullheaded, and he's going to say what he wants to say even if it's not exactly respectful. Don't pay him any mind."

"It's easier to ignore him and what he's saying if I'm not staying in his house. I'm fine, ma. I love you." Gia walked past her mother and opened the front door.

She often got tired of her mother saying the same things over and over whenever Blake made Gia or her sister angry. They shouldn't have to ignore him or just accept that's how he was. Blake was old enough to learn some decorum. He still liked to speak to his daughters like they were children sometimes, and neither one of them appreciated it because they were grown, out of his house, and taking care of themselves. Blake acted as if Gia was a minor, and she met Money when he was a grown man. The way Blake was against their relationship, maybe he did know something that she didn't know, but why not lovingly let her learn on her own and be there to comfort her if the relationship failed. He had basically told her he didn't give a damn.

Once she was inside her Kia, Gia texted Havanna praying that she was at home. Her friend had a very hectic work schedule sometimes, and she might have to work seven or eight days in a row before she got a day off. When Havanna responded a minute later and told Gia she was at home, a sigh of relief was breathed. Gia started her car and headed in the direction of Havanna's home. It was just Havanna and her daughter Kendall in the home but last year, Havanna had bought a four bedroom house. She loved being a nurse, but she worked hard as hell, and Havanna would be damned if she didn't enjoy the fruit of her labor. She had a very nice and cozy guest bedroom set up, and Gia knew she'd be welcomed there until she could get a place. She wasn't even supposed to be driving, but she was getting the hell away from Blake.

Havanna's house was in a posh neighborhood not too far from the suburbs that Gia's parents lived in, so she arrived in no time. She had been anxious to get to her friend's home, so she hadn't explained the nature of her visit to Havanna.

"Hey, baby." Gia smiled at Kendall when she opened the door for her.

Kendall gave Gia a one-armed hug. "Hi, auntie Gia."

Havanna was sitting on the couch on her laptop. She glanced up to speak to her friend and saw the overnight bag in her hand. "Uh oh. What did Blake do?"

Gia chuckled finding it funny that Havanna knew exactly which parent it was that had sent her running. "He told me in so many words that if Money loses his next fight because I broke up with him, he'll disown me. That's what I took from it."

Havanna's brows lifted, and she sat up. She parted her lips to speak but glanced over at Kendall who was on her iPad. The seven-year-old appeared to be engrossed in Tik Tok, but Havanna could never be too sure. She was old school, and she didn't believe in talking about grown folk things in the presence of her daughter.

"Let's step in the kitchen. Can you drink wine?"

Gia stood up and followed her friend. "I haven't had any pain medication in more than six hours, so I think it should be fine. Hell, I've seen people chase pain medication with liquor and then smoke a blunt, so I don't think I'll die."

Havanna inhaled a deep breath. "Okay, when you texted me from the hospital and told me that Money had indeed gone to London, I didn't speak on it because your man your business. But you're really ending it with him?" She asked as she grabbed a bottle of wine from her wine rack and then pulled a drawer open for the corkscrew.

Gia's parents had a very nice home. It was damn near a mansion. Money didn't have a mansion, but his townhouse was brand new when he moved in. Very modern with new top of the line appliances, so Gia was used to nice homes, but she loved being in Havanna's house because she knew the story behind it. A lot of people wrote her off when she got pregnant in high school, but Havanna had beaten the odds and completed college. Not only that, she was a damn good nurse, and she had purchased her $450,000 house without the help of a man. Kendall's sorry ass daddy didn't even pay child support. Everything Havanna had, she worked hard for it. Shit, Gia didn't even have kids, and her friend was doing better than her.

"I really am. It's not *just* London, but London was the straw that broke the camel's back. No man is or will ever be perfect, but if Money was putting forth some effort, I would have continued to fight for my relationship with everything in me. I just refuse to be the only one fighting. I don't think he wants to be in a relationship, and I'm going to have enough pride to let him go."

"Are you okay?" Havanna passed Gia a glass of wine knowing deep down there was no way Gia was okay. She loved Money's ass.

"Not really, but I will be." Gia didn't want to lie to her friend, but she didn't want to come across as completely pathetic either. Havanna didn't have to know all the specifics of her grieving process. Gia had been crying every day, and she knew she'd probably still be crying a week from now. It was just a process that she'd have to endure and get through.

"And he doesn't know?" Havanna sipped her wine.

"No. He's texted me twice since he's been gone. I ignored both text messages, and he hasn't called. Money doesn't like to hash things out. When I'm mad at him he'll avoid me for a few days and then when he thinks enough time has passed, he'll come trying to talk to me about something stupid like the weather. I'm sure he feels if he calls, I'll start nagging and ruin his trip. He doesn't even know that I was in the hospital or that I had surgery."

Havanna's eyes narrowed. "That nigga makes my ass itch. See, I tried to be a mature adult and not talk bad about him but how is he avoiding you when he's the one that did wrong? I hate grown ass men that can't communicate."

"All I really have at his place are tons of clothes, shoes, and purses. I bought some of the décor that he has now, but I'm not taking that. He can keep it. I have a lot of things, so I'll probably rent a small storage unit just for a month until I can find a place."

"You know I have so many clothes and shoes that my master bedroom closet is full and so is the closet in one of the extra bedrooms, but you can put your things in the guest room and the garage. Don't rent a storage unit if you don't have to. And you know you're more than welcome to stay here until you get a place. I hate that you're going through a heartbreak, but I'm glad you are finally realizing that nigga doesn't deserve you."

Gia didn't respond. She took a large sip of wine instead. She appreciated Havanna's words of encouragement but nothing her friend said was going to stop her heart from feeling as if it was shattering.

***

Azon watched Fallon hold onto the edge of the pool while she paddled her legs behind her. "You sure you don't want to get in?" she asked him with a coy smile on her face.

Fallon and Azon had three phone conversations since he met her at the racetrack and on this day, he'd come to her apartment complex to hang out by the pool with her.

"Nah, that's all you. I can sit back and enjoy the show though."

Fallon looked great in her red two piece, and the fruity alcoholic beverage that she'd brought with her had her loose and flirtatious. Azon felt that he knew enough about her, so if she chose to give him some their first time hanging out, he wouldn't turn it down, and he wouldn't judge her. He was horny as hell, but he was going to wait and see where things went. He hadn't come to her place with the intentions of trying to crack on her but in the last hour that he'd been there, she'd made it subtly clear that she was attracted to him.

Fallon picked up her flask and drank the last of her beverage. She climbed the stairs and got out of the pool. With beads of water dripping off her body, she made her way over to the empty lounge chair beside Azon and picked up her towel. "I need a refill on my drink, and I'd rather sip it in a nice, air conditioned apartment. Care to join me?"

"I can do that," Azon's eyes trailed the length of her toned body. Azon stood up and adjusted his stiff dick in his black cargo shorts and followed her the short distance to her building. Inside her second-floor apartment, he had to admit that the aesthetic of her place fit her. There were plants in every corner and in front of the window. She had a lot of African paintings and statues. The living room was full of bright colors, and she had a large bookshelf filled with books.

Azon could tell she was a free spirit, but she was smart and took care of business also, and he liked that about her. He wasn't trying to rush anything with anybody but so far, Fallon hadn't done anything to turn him off from wanting to get to know her. He sat down on the couch, and his eyes fell on an ashtray.

"You smoke?" He wondered why he'd never asked her that before.

"Yeah. I don't think I'm a pothead, but I do smoke one joint a day."

"I can smoke in here?"

"Sure. I don't like cigars. I only smoke joints, but you can smoke while I take a shower and watch this chlorine off."

"Bet."

She went to take a shower, and he rolled the blunt that he'd been fiending for. Azon started smoking weed when he was sixteen, and it had been up ever since. He needed a blunt to start his day, another mid-day, and one before bed. Azon smoked that good stuff, so he remained high for three to four hours each time he smoked. He saw no need to keep smoking when he was only going to get but so high. He knew a lot of people chain smoked out of habit, but Azon smoked to get high. On a super long day he might smoke four blunts in a day, but it generally wasn't more than that. He didn't mind being sober for short periods of time. Azon hadn't gotten to the point where he had to be high every second of every day. Being a naturally calm and laid back person, it wasn't like weed altered his personality much anyway.

The only real difference he saw was that weed gave him way more patience than he had when he was sober. As he lit the blunt, Azon saw that Gia had sent him a text message asking if he could do her a favor in the next few hours. The shower was still running, so Azon called her. He wouldn't have done so in front of Fallon, but she was occupied, so he didn't see the harm. Gia answered on the third ring.

"What's good?" Azon's voice was strained because he was holding weed smoke in his lungs.

"Hey. So, I want to go to Money's place and move my things out before he gets home tomorrow. The only problem is I can't lift anything heavy. I've carried a few trash bags, but even that is pushing it because they're large bags that are filled to capacity. I have boxes left at the house, and I just wanted to know if you could move them. I'm not speaking to my father at the moment, and my best friend is at work. I'd also never invite you to another man's house if I thought some shit would go down, but Money is out of the country."

Azon refrained from telling her that he wasn't scared of that nigga. If he wasn't out of the country, and she needed her shit, he'd go get it. "Yeah, I can do that. I can text you when I'm ready to head in your direction, and you can give me the address," he pulled from the blunt again.

"Thank you so much, Azon. I really appreciate it. I just want all of my things out of his home before he gets back."

"No problem."

That phone call made Azon aware that Gia seemed serious about leaving Money. Speaking of money, Azon had been getting to it, so he hadn't had a lot of time to talk to Gia. He did make it his business to at least check on her throughout the day, since he knew she was recovering. Azon took a few more pulls of the blunt, and he thought he was high and tripping when Fallon sauntered into the room naked. She saw him do a double take, and she giggled.

"Just a small disclaimer. I love being naked. It doesn't have a lot to do with you in particular. I hate wearing clothes. My real friends have seen my body almost as much as I have."

"I'm not complaining at all." Azon saw that she was one of those real natural chicks that either didn't shave at all or that didn't shave often. She didn't have a bush, but there was some hair on her vagina. He didn't mind though. Azon didn't give a damn about hair as long as there wasn't an odor. He'd smelled some pungent vaginas that were hairless.

Fallon walked into the kitchen and refreshed her glass. When she walked back into the living room, she sat beside him on the couch and sipped while he smoked. She grabbed her remote from the coffee table and turned some music on. Soothing sounds with a Summer Walker slash Erykah Badu vibe filled the room. Azon discreetly looked around the room for any signs that might make him uncomfortable. He was Haitian and used to being judged and stereotyped, and he didn't want to do it with other people, but he wasn't stupid. All he needed was a sign that she was one of those self-proclaimed witches that did love spells and shit, and he was gon' be the fuck out. Azon didn't play with hoodoo, voodoo, none of that shit.

If he even had the slightest notion that she was doing some off the wall shit, he'd cut her ass off with the quickness, and if he had to contact any of his aunties in Haiti to assist him with some shit that she might think was a good idea to put on him, she was going to regret it. By the time Fallon was done with her drink, Azon was finished with his blunt, and they both had heavy lids and were feeling good.

"So, Mr. New In Town, you haven't dealt with any other females since you've been here? Not that it matters, but I can show you my STD results from a few months ago. I haven't had sex in ten months, and I really want to have sex with you. Like real bad."

Azon chuckled. "Real bad, huh?

Fallon nodded, and Azon placed the last of his blunt in her ashtray. Azon wasn't a big fan of kissing people in the mouth unless he fucked with them like that so needless to say, he hadn't engaged in a good, sloppy tongue kiss in so long that he could barely remember it. He moved over slightly and began sucking on Fallon's neck. Since she was already naked, he pinched her nipple gently as he assaulted the flesh of her neck with his tongue. He hadn't been with anyone since he'd come to town, but he ignored the question because it wasn't her business.

"I want to taste you," Fallon moaned, and Azon knew in that moment she really was a freak, and he was going to have some fun with her.

"That's something you can do without even letting me know, baby," Azon peered at her lustfully.

Fallon gave him a wicked grin and within seconds, she had lowered her body and was freeing his dick from the confinement of his boxer briefs. Azon was already harder than Chinese arithmetic, and Fallon eyed his manhood with a gleam in her eyes. Azon's penis was nothing less than a work of art, and she was enthralled. Her mouth watered, and Fallon took Azon into her moist mouth causing him to push out a deep moan. She had barely started sucking, and her mouth felt divine on his member. Azon stared down at her thick locs, beautifully melanated skin, and her alluring scent. Shorty smelled of lavender and a hint of mango. Azon knew sex with her would be amazing because women like her didn't play about drinking water and eating fruits and vegetables. She probably drank all kinds of herbal teas and detoxed on a regular basis. He knew that pussy would be wet as fuck if nothing else.

"Do that shit," Azon coached in a deep whisper as Fallon made love to his dick with her mouth.

She gagged, spit, hummed, and provided the ultimate pleasure.

"Now, I want to feel him," she peered up at Azon with a naughty gleam in her eyes, and her subtle aggressiveness turned him on. Fallon was a woman that knew what she wanted, and she didn't front about it. He could dig that.

Azon reached into his pocket for a condom. "Just tell me how you want it, baby."

"I want it from the back with you pulling my locs and calling me a nasty bitch."

Azon's brows lifted, and a smirk eased across his face. "Say less."

Fallon rose up with a smile on her face and after Azon covered his penis with a Magnum, he stood up while she got in position on the couch. He ran a finger down her center and found that Fallon's peach was dripping with nectar.

"You ready for this dick, huh?" he marveled as he rubbed her clit gently.

"Yes. I want it so bad," Fallon moaned.

Azon placed kisses on her spine while he stroked her nub. He spread her cheeks and pushed the head of his dick into her tight opening.

"Yesssss," she moaned just from the head of his dick being inside of her.

Azon grabbed a handful of her locs aggressively and jerked her head back while pushing himself deeper into her. "I'm 'bout to give you what you want. Make sure you ready for this shit," he breathed as he pushed all of himself into her.

Fallon's body trembled, and she moaned like a wounded animal. Azon gritted his teeth together, got a good grip on her hair, and he pounded in and out of her savagely. Within moments, she was convulsing as she came, and the way her honeypot squeezed Azon's member made him release a guttural moan. He smacked her ass with three hard slaps that had Fallon losing her mind. Nectar ran down her thighs and she spread her own ass cheeks wide allowing Azon deeper access.

"This fuckin' pussy good," he growled.

Fallon eased off the couch, bent over, and gripped her ankles. "You a nasty ass bitch for real." If that's how she liked to get her rocks off, Azon had no issue with talking dirty to her. "You take this dick like a good lil' slut. Putian," he cursed in French as their bodies smacked together.

"Please let me ride it," Fallon begged, and Azon backed out of her.

He sat down on the couch and Fallon straddled him and buried her face in the crook of her his neck as she rode him hard and fast. "This is the best dick I have ever had," Fallon whimpered.

Azon was slightly shocked because he hadn't even turned all the way up on her, but if she said it was the best maybe that was so. "Word?" he asked. "Ride this dick like it's the best you ever had then." He slapped her ass again. "Sit up straight and get this nut up out a nigga," he demanded.

Fallon threw her head back and did as Azon requested. Minutes later, his hand was wrapped back in her locs as he sucked on her neck and erupted into the condom. Both their chests heaved up and down as they attempted to catch their breath. Finally, she stood up and looked at him with glossed over eyes.

"That was fucking amazing." She sauntered into the bathroom and came back with a warm rag to clean him up with.

As soon as she was done, he stood up and started getting dressed, so he could go help Gia and spend the rest of his day making money. "I'll definitely be in touch." Azon assured her, and she walked him to the door.

In the car, he texted Gia for the address, so he could get her things up out of Money's crib.

Eight

Gia's breathing stalled when she opened the door and saw Azon standing in front of her. She wasn't sure how it was possible that he seemed to get finer and finer. "What's going on pretty lady," he asked, and she gave him a small smile.

"Ready to get off my feet. The boxes are upstairs. I wasn't able to carry them down. They should all fit in my vehicle." Whether he was out of the country or not, Gia didn't want Azon in Money's house longer than he had to be.

She led him up the stairs and despite having just had sex less than an hour before, his eyes zeroed in on her ass as it jiggled with each step that she took. Azon was focused on Gia's body, but he'd seen enough to know that Money was living aight. For all the fights he had under his belt and the endorsement deals that he had, Azon had expected a little more but at the end of the day, he didn't really give a fuck how or where the next man was living. Gia showed him where the boxes were, and he took them out to her Kia one at a time. After five trips to the car, he was done. With a heavy heart, Gia locked the townhouse and left the key in the mailbox. She would text Money later and let him know it was there.

While she locked the door, Azon walked over to her car and leaned against it. "You got somebody to get your boxes out of the car when you get to where you're going?"

"Yeah. I'm staying with my best friend until I can get a place, and I park my car in her garage. She can get them when she gets off later, or they can stay in there until tomorrow. They aren't heavy. I'm just crippled at the moment," she smiled nervously. Azon was peering at her intently as if she was the most interesting person in the world, and she was only talking about some boxes.

"How you been feeling though? You okay?" He seemed genuinely concerned, and that warmed Gia's aching heart.

"I'm okay." It didn't take Gia long to learn that constantly saying she was okay when she wasn't was draining, but she refused to sulk, mope, and be sad all damn day. "How have you been? Are you okay?"

"Every day above ground with money in my pocket and food in my belly is a good day, shawty. How long you gon' be crippled and shit? I'm trying to take you out on a date."

On more than one occasion, Gia had thought about doing ungodly things with Azon, but that was a daydream. A frequent fantasy. It was nice to think about, but when the opportunity to make it a reality presented itself, she immediately became nervous.

"Do you think that's a good idea? I'm fresh out of a relationship. Like super fresh."

A slight scowl appeared on Azon's face. "What that mean to me? You single, right? I know how you ladies like to sit around and listen to sad music while you drink wine and heal and shit but fuck all that. Just because that nigga didn't know what to do with you, I can't take you out to eat or to a movie, maybe bowling, or to a museum or something?"

"A museum?" her perfectly arched brow lifted. "What you know about museums, nigga?" she joked.

Azon ran his tongue across his teeth. "Don't let the hair, the fronts, and the swag fool you. A nigga done been to the opera before. Don't sleep on me. A man like me can change your life. You just gotta stop being scared and let me do the damn thing."

Gia cleared her throat nervously. "Ain't nobody scared of you." She wasn't too comfortable talking about dates and flirting in front of Money's place, so she decided to go ahead and wrap the conversation up. "Just call me or text me about that date. I should be all the way good in another week."

Azon's eyes trailed the length of her body, and he took in her gray sundress, her orange Tory Burch sandals, and the cropped denim jacket that she wore. Fresh, freckle decorated face, and juicy kissable lips that were covered in peach lip gloss. The gold watch on her wrist and the large gold hoops in her ears made the outfit pop a little more, and she smelled good as always. Azon didn't know shit about perfume, but shorty smelled, soft and feminine with a hint of spice.

"Bet. I'll call you about the date in a week, but I'll talk to you later when you let me know you made it in safely." Azon pulled at the fabric that was clinging to her belly before walking off leaving her standing there smiling.

Once she was inside her vehicle, Gia blew out a slow, steady breath. Why did she have to put a time limit on hanging out with him? They weren't getting married or having a kid. They had already flirted on many occasions and had a few conversations. What would be the harm in grabbing a bite to eat with him? At least she could do it freely and not feel guilty that she was cheating on her man because she no longer had one. That reminded her. Gia sucked in a sharp breath before unlocking her phone and texting Money. She figured she may as well get it over with.

She had already changed his contact name from *Bae* to *Money*. Her fingers moved swiftly as she said everything she wanted to say. There was no need to send a super long, detailed message. If he'd been listening to her for the past year, then he would fully understand why she left. Before she hit send, Gia's eyes scanned the words to make sure she hadn't left anything out.

I left. Your key is in the mailbox, and I've already had my mail forwarded to my new address. Things aren't the same, but I'm sure you know that. I'm also sure that if you cared, you would have tried to change a long time ago. I think we both outgrew the relationship, and that's okay. I wish you all the best.

With tears in her eyes, she sent the message and blocked Money's number. She then blocked him on social media before backing out of his driveway. Two years down the drain, but that was life. One of her employees had recently ended a ten-year relationship. Gia couldn't fathom being with someone for that long and then waking up one day and he wasn't there anymore. She would have certainly rather wasted two years than ten. Everyone wasn't as lucky as her mother. Blake was Lauren's high school sweetheart. She'd only been with one guy before him and no others since him. She rocked his ring, donned his last name, and carried four of his children, though two of her pregnancies ended in miscarriage. Gia wasn't sure if her father had ever cheated on her mother, but she didn't care to know.

What she did know was that for as blunt and insensitive as her father could be sometimes, no one could check him like Lauren could. He could be a jerk with everyone else, but all she had to do was shoot an irritated glance his way, and he'd simmer all the way down. If Lauren wanted something, she never had to ask twice and if that's not the kind of man that wanted to be with her, then Gia would rather be single. Wanting to feel loved, appreciated, and secure in a relationship should never be an issue. She and Money didn't have kids together, and they weren't married. Those things made walking away a little easier, and Gia told herself that she'd be okay.

When Gia arrived at Havanna's house, she let herself in with the key that her friend had given her, and she went to the guest bedroom, and pulled a notebook and a pen from her overnight bag. Since she didn't want to sit on the bed in her outside clothes, and she wasn't going back out, Gia took a quick shower, and changed into some leggings and a tank top. She sat in the center of the bed Indian style and opened the journal. Yes, she had the boutique, but it was time to put some other plans in motion. Gia was going to put all of the energy that she'd put into her relationship into this new chapter of her life. She'd have a new place to live, new furniture, and she needed a new source of income.

Lowkey, she was almost excited to see what was waiting for her on the other side of this journey. *New dick.* The thought crept into her mind making her shake her head. Azon was for sure going to be an interesting plot twist to the story, but she damn sure couldn't let it get her off track. If Gia didn't remember anything else, she knew she needed to remember to keep her head in the game.

***

Azon paid for the three pairs of sneakers that he'd purchased and stepped aside so Islande could pay for the shoes he'd picked out. After a long day of hustling, the men linked up at home and decided to hit the mall before it closed. They were then going to stop and get some drinks and food from a popular sports bar. Azon loved being an entrepreneur because he lived every day like it was Friday. He didn't give a damn if it was Tuesday. If he wanted to hang out late, get drunk, and bullshit, that's what he did. He wasn't a complete free spirit because he did like having some structure. No matter how late he stayed out, Azon always made it a habit to get up before the temperature got too high and get a workout in. He loved working out outside. Being from Florida, that was an option year round, and he knew if he was still in North Carolina during the winter months, that's something he'd have to get used to. Working out outside in temperatures below sixty degrees would never be his thing. Being disciplined in that way made Azon feel a little better about life. He liked knowing that he could reach goals and push through even on the days he didn't feel like it.

The brothers were going to link with Fabienne at the sports bar. Islande paid for his shoes, and the brothers headed for the exit because they'd already purchased clothes. Clothes and shoes were something that Azon had never been too pressed to spend money on. He could be the plainest nigga in the room and pull the baddest chick in the room, but he was making money on a daily basis and plenty of it. Why not enjoy it? He still hadn't splurged on any pricy jewelry, but in due time. Azon had three separate stashes that he added to daily. He had the money he was saving in case of an emergency like being arrested, needing a lawyer, needing to get out of town ASAP, etc. His second stash was for his next re-up because it was too easy to blow through the money that you're making when a lot of so called hustlers didn't realize that all the money you make back isn't profit unless you don't plan to re-up again. And the third stash he had was for when he decided to really go all out and get on his big boy shit.

The Camaro was nice. It was nice as fuck. But the more money he made, Azon knew he would want to upgrade his life more and more. Azon wasn't used to the kind of money that he was making in Diamond Cove, but he was still determined to be smart with it. He didn't have to worry about sending any money to his parents because they would never take his dirty money. He could tell them that he had a job, and they'd ask to see his pay stubs. Azon's parents didn't trust a thing he said and since his father had no problem paying his bills and providing for his wife, Azon wouldn't try to force his money on them. His sister was a different story, however. She didn't give a damn where the money came from and as a college student, she always needed something. Earlier, Azon had cash apped her $500, and the day before, Islande had sent her $500. It was unheard of for Angeline to receive $1,000 in two days. Her parents did what they could, but she was used to getting less than $300 a month from them and all of that went towards food.

Islande and Azon swore Angeline to secrecy, but she knew their parents well enough that she'd never tell them how much money her brothers were sending her anyway. Her father would take his phone herself and send any money that was left right back. If there was a picture beside the definition of pride in the dictionary, Michael's face would have been it.

On the ride home, Azon and Islande's conversation consisted of everything from the money they were making, the different women they'd encountered, and the kind of car that Islande was planning on getting. By the time Azon pulled up at the house, both men were hungry as hell, and they wasted no time getting dressed and heading right back out to go to the sports bar. The place they decided to go was only about ten minutes from their house, and Fabienne beat them there. When they approached the bar where he was seated, the men all gave each other dap. The place wasn't packed, but there was a nice sized crowd. Azon could immediately pick up on the fact that Fabienne seemed agitated. His brows were furrowed, and his lips were set in a tight line.

"Somebody texted you and said they missed their period?" Azon joked as he took a seat on the barstool next to Fabienne.

Fabienne chuckled. "If Khloe doesn't leave me alone, I'm going to jail, bro. You know I'd die behind my sister. If a man puts his hands on Jeanne, he'd have to see me. But yo," Fabienne shook his head. "Men that brag about beating women are suckas in my opinion, but I want to do that broad so dirty."

Islande shook his head. "Don't do it. Just pay Jeanne to whoop her. Your sister has some hands, and I know she'll do it for some bread."

"She's threatening to do it for free because Khloe keeps going to my mom's crib."

Azon's brows hiked up. "Oh, shawty trying to get hurt for real because where the fuck you think Jeanne got her hands from? Johanne nice with her shit too. She's the sweetest lady ever, but she don't play 'bout her kids."

"And that's what's pissing me off because my mom doesn't bother anyone. You'll see drama in a church parking lot before you see it at my mom's house. But that broad has come over there twice yelling all in my face and shit being all loud. The next time she puts her hands on me, go ahead and call me a sucka, 'cus I'm rocking her shit."

"Shorty really think you gon' fuck with her after she fucked your man? She can't know you for real to ever think you'd let that slide."

"Swear to God," Fabienne co-signed tossing back the rest of his drink. "Shorty tried to play me like I was slow as fuck. When I told her I wanted my own place, she cried talking about how she held me down for two years, and I won't even live with her. She was pouring it on thick like she really stood ten toes down for a nigga, and she actually had me feeling guilty. She almost got me." Fabienne chuckled angrily because he felt stupid for ever trusting her. He cringed thinking of all the times they'd given each other sloppy tongue kisses, and she had sucked his homie's dick. Just thinking about it had Fabienne's body warm with anger.

"At least you found out."

"And I was mad, but I'm good. You'd think I'd be the one popping up at her crib acting an ass. I haven't tried to fight Sabien. I haven't called Khloe. I'm trying to walk away from her as peacefully as I can, and she won't leave well enough alone. The last bitch I fucked before making it official with Khloe got me jumped by her lame ass baby daddy and his cousin. Now, this hoe fucked my friend while I was locked up. My judgement is terrible, and I'll never take another broad serious."

The bartender came over, and Azon and Islande ordered their drinks. Azon didn't have any advice to give his cousin on love. He'd never been in love, and he'd handle a female like Khloe the same way that Fabienne was. The alcohol was lightening Fabienne's mood and soon, the men were watching the game on the mounted televisions above the bar engaging in conversation about more pleasant matters like Fabienne wanting to purchase a motorcycle. They had just asked the bartender for the tab when something or someone caught Fabienne's eye, and the way his posture instantly became rigid, Azon knew it was about to be some shit.

He followed the direction of Fabienne's gaze, and he saw that his cousin was glowering at a group of three men that were laughing and talking amongst each other. Azon had to wonder if one of the men was Sabien. He could practically feel the heat coming off of his cousin.

"What's good, brother?"

Fabienne's jaw muscles clenched, and his orbs never left the men. "The nigga in the red is the punk ass nigga that was with Taj when they jumped me at ole girl's house. I'll never forget that face as long as I live," Fabienne seethed.

It was up. No questions asked. All three men stood and paid their tabs. Fabienne headed in the direction of the group, and Azon unclasped the watch on his wrist and eased it into his pocket. It wasn't a Rolex or a Patek, but he knew there was a possibility that he was about to get real active, and he didn't want to risk it coming off. Azon knew he had to be careful because his hands were lethal and not in a 'that nigga can fight' way. Azon could beat a man to death without trying too hard. Once he was turned up, it was hard to turn him down, so he tried to refrain from going there. He'd almost rather just shoot a nigga than do anyone dirty with his fists because it could get just that gruesome. He knew Fabienne could no doubt hold his own, and Azon and Islande would mostly be there to make sure Fabienne didn't once again get jumped.

Fabienne wasn't with all the talking but just as he did with Taj, he didn't want to sneak his opponent. He wanted that nigga to know what was up and to prepare himself. Fabienne never had to do a sneak attack in his life to get the upper hand in a fight.

"You remember me, pussy?" Fabienne wedged himself in between the group of friends and stepped into the personal space of Taj's cousin.

Fabienne was the biggest of his group, but Azon and Islande looked equally menacing, biceps bulging or not. The man who Fabienne approached was caught off guard and while he wanted to be gangsta, something was telling him that his ass was about to be grass. His brother couldn't fight for shit, and his friend was a fireman that didn't do the public spectacles of embarrassment. If the people he was with couldn't diffuse the situation, he might be on his own.

"Nah, I don't know you, homie." The guy took a step back from Fabienne and backed into a table that was directly behind him.

Fabienne took a step forward placing himself right back into the man's personal space. "You probably don't know me seeing as how you and your pussy ass cousin Taj snuck me from behind at his baby mama's house. It's me, nigga. The one y'all jumped from behind while I was drunk and in some pussy, and you beat the fuck out of me. But I want to see if you can do that shit again." The rage dancing in his dark eyes almost made Chris urinate on himself.

He had never won a fight in his life and when he got the chance to beat Fabienne to a pulp with Taj, he felt empowered. He felt that he'd actually done something, but he had no clue it would come back to bite him in the ass. Even with he and Taj both beating Fabienne, the man got himself together fairly quickly and was giving them a run for their money until Taj hit him with a lamp. If he could handle the two of them at a time like that, Chris knew he was surely about to get his ass handed to him in the middle of a semi-packed bar. He inwardly prayed that security would come fast as hell.

"Th-that was a while ago," Chris stammered. He hated that he was stuttering, but he'd rather be embarrassed in that way than by getting beat up out in public. He had seen first-hand what Fabienne did to Taj once he caught up with him. "I was with my c-cousin, and he had beef, so I was helped him but.."

"Nah, no but's, nigga," Fabienne smirked. "I just wanted you to know that you about to get yo' ass beat. I didn't ask for explanations or excuses." Before he could finish talking good, Fabienne cocked his arm back and hit Chris so hard that the man flew backwards over the small table he was leaning against.

The guys he was with took a step forward, and Azon spoke to the one nearest him. "I wouldn't do that if I was you."

Islande didn't want to talk. He simply hit the other man with a two-piece that instantly halted his steps. The man whirled around so fast that he tripped over his own foot, and when he saw the devilish smirk on Islande's face, he knew he wanted no parts. When he didn't attempt to fight back, Islande refrained from hitting him again. Islande didn't feel bad for hitting him because the nigga was guilty by association.

Fabienne was beating Chris like a man possessed. For as much as Taj and his cousin mangled Fabienne's face when they jumped him, Chris wasn't even fighting back. Fabienne was throwing punches faster than a person could blink, and every one of them was connecting with his opponent's face. Azon's phone vibrated in his pocket, but he wouldn't dare take his eyes off the fight to check his phone. Four employees of the bar headed in the direction of the fight, and Islande and Azon both stepped in front of the men.

"Don't touch my muhfuckin' people," Azon growled while Islande went over to pull Fabienne off the man that was no longer moving.

Fabienne could see that the person he'd beaten was still breathing, so he knew the man wasn't dead. He still decided to get out of dodge before the police came, because he wasn't trying to do another two years in prison behind this goofy ass nigga. The men left the bar.

Fabienne headed in one direction, and the brothers headed in another. Azon tossed his brother his car keys.

"You can drive, nigga. I'm always the one chauffeuring you around like I'm an Uber driver or some shit."

Islande didn't mind driving. He couldn't wait until he got his own car. He got rental cars here and there, but he was ready to purchase his own. He missed the robbery with Nice, so his fortune wasn't as large as Fabienne and Azon's was, but he was far from broke. He was still trying to decide between a Camaro or a McLaren. Islande loved fast cars. Within the next year, his goal was to have a Bugatti because they could go up to 253 mph. A Bugatti was a little out of his price range at the moment and not only that, a Bugatti wasn't an every day car. For now, he wanted something that he could drive every day. When he got the Bugatti that would be the car he only pulled out on special occasions.

Once he was nestled in the passenger seat, Azon took the time to check his phone, and he saw that it was Gia that had texted him. He responded back to her, and they had causal conversation the entire way to his house. Once Islande arrived home, it dawned on Azon that with the drinks in his system, he wanted to see Gia's pretty ass face. He texted and asked her if he could pull up.

"I'm not coming in to stay. You can leave the car running. I'm just stepping in to grab my weed, so I can sit here and roll a blunt," he informed Islande. Gia hadn't even responded to his text message, but if she wasn't up for company, he'd hit Fallon up. Azon had thought about that good ass pussy a few times since they had sex.

He definitely wanted to sample that when he was drunk. High sex was cool, but drunk sex with the right person was unmatched. Azon was far from a minute man but with alcohol in his system, he was sure to last at least fifteen minutes longer than usual. And when the woman was inebriated as well, she made those extra minutes heavenly. Azon had settled back into his car and was in the process of rolling a blunt when Gia texted back the address of her friend's home. Azon finished rolling his blunt, lit it, took a few tokes, then texted her back that he was on his way. Once the address was inserted into his GPS, he saw that he was almost twenty minutes away from her. He knew by the time he reached his destination; he'd be good and high. Some money called his phone, but shop was closed for the night.

Azon's mind wandered aimlessly as he drove through the city of Diamond Cove. At twenty-five, he had no idea where he wanted to plant his roots. Would he go back to Florida at some point or remain here? Did he want kids and if so, how many? Did he want to get married or just have kids with someone that he loved deeply? Azon had been playing life by ear. He'd been waking up every day only focused on that day, and he wondered if it was time for that to change. Buy a house in one or two years, leave the game and put some babies up in somebody. He had no clue the direction that he wanted his life to go in. By the time he pulled up to where Gia was, not one of the questions he'd pondered on had an answer. Azon picked his phone up to let Gia know he had arrived. Once the message was sent, his orbs scanned the homes in the neighborhood, and he gave an appreciative nod. The garage door that he was parked in front of lifted, and Gia made an appearance. Donned in black sweatpants and a black, fitted, belly shirt, she looked beautiful as she always did. White sneakers adorned her feet, and her braids were up in a bun with the baby hairs laid. Even in the dark, Azon could see the diamond studs dancing in her ears and when she got inside his car, the aroma of jasmine and sandalwood filled his nostrils.

"You look like you feel very good," she smiled at him as she noticed his chinky eyes. Azon was already sexy, but he was sexier to her when his eyes were damn near slits.

His cheeks lifted into a smile. "I feel good as fuck, and I match how you look." He licked his lips, and Gia's face immediately turned red.

"Thank you, but I have on dusty ass sweats and sneakers. I'll take the compliment though."

A silence filled the car that was almost awkward to her yet comforting to Azon. He gazed at her for a moment, becoming lost in her beauty. "So about that date."

Gia erupted into laughter. "It has not been a week, Azon."

He loved the way she said his name. Her southern drawl was different from the southern drawl of Floridians. It was sexy to Azon. So sexy that his dick was hardening.

"We can plan it for six days from now, but you look fine to me. We don't have to do any strenuous activities. All you have to do is sit and look pretty. The same way you are now. You tell me when you want to go, where you want to go, and the time you want to go, and I'm there."

Gia pondered for a moment. "There's this really nice Thai restaurant that just opened up last month. It's always pretty packed, and you can't get in right now without reservations. I can make reservations for next Saturday at six PM."

"You do that. You just been chilling every day?"

Gia rolled her eyes. "Yes, and it's killing me. I'm not in a lot of pain though, so I'm stopping by my boutique tomorrow. I've been away for too many days, and I trust my employees but at the same time, I don't. Nobody will care about your shit the way you do. I'm almost nervous about what I might walk in on because I'm very meticulous about my business."

"As you should be. I'm sure it's cool. You're probably just being extra because it is your business."

"I also need to look at some apartments. I love my friend's house, and being here with her and her daughter is nice, but I know I have to get the ball rolling on finding a place. I'm excited. I've never lived on my own. I went straight from my parents' house to Money's place."

"You don't have to live on your own. You can move in with me," Azon joked, but his expression remained serious, and Gia found herself squeezing her thighs together to calm her yoni down. She was baffled at how Azon's head was resting against the seat. He wasn't moving, and his drawl was slow and lazy, and she was more aroused than she'd been in a long time.

"Someone else paying the rent does sound nice, but I have to be a big girl and do it on my own," she smiled.

Before Azon could respond, the bright headlights of a car pulling up behind Azon's shone through the car, and Gia turned to look over her shoulder. She knew it wasn't Havanna, because she was already inside. And she hadn't said anything about having company. When Gia realized that it was Money pulling up, her heart fell into her ass.

"Oh my God. That's my ex." Gia knew enough to know that Azon would never be afraid of Money. She could also tell he was a different breed than Money, so while Money could hold his own, an altercation between them was the last thing she wanted.

"Oh yeah?" Azon replied in a bored tone, and Gia's eyes darted back to his face.

"Please let me handle this. I don't know what he wants, and I'm sure he's been a couple of places looking for me before he figured that I was here. I'll tell him to move his car, so you can leave."

Azon could see the fear in her eyes as they danced back and forth across his face, and he hoped she wasn't scared for him. Shit, she didn't even have to be afraid for herself because Money wasn't going to do shit to her in his presence. "He doesn't have to move his car. I'm good. Unless you want me to go," he replied as Money got out of his vehicle.

Azon had tinted windows, so Money wouldn't have been able to see in the car. However, Gia didn't want him ringing the bell and waking Havanna and Kendall, so she got out of the car without replying to Azon.

"What are you doing here, Money?" she tried to sound confident, but Gia was shitting bricks.

He eyed the car before looking in her face. "This is the same car that was at my house. I saw the shit on the cameras. You had another nigga in my house, Gia?!" His voice rose an octave higher than normal, but Azon remained in the car. His eyes were trained on Money, but he'd let Gia handle her own shit until he felt like she couldn't.

"My appendix ruptured, and I had to have emergency surgery. I couldn't lift the boxes, and he was the only person that could come. As you could see from the footage, he wasn't there long, and I didn't do anything inappropriate."

Money's head jerked back, and he scoffed. "You didn't do anything inappropriate. You had another nigga in my crib!"

"Stop yelling before someone calls the police," she hissed. "This is a quiet neighborhood. Don't bring your drama over here, Money."

"Nah fuck that," he stepped closer to her while Azon's nostrils began to flare. "That's the nigga from the gym. You don't know that nigga, so how did you and him become so buddy buddy all of a sudden that you felt bold enough to invite that nigga to my crib?" Money's eyes were dark and soulless as he inched closer into Gia's face, and Azon had enough.

He emerged from the car. "That nigga is right here, homie. My name is Azon, and I've asked her out countless times despite knowing she fucked with your pussy ass. She turned me down each and every time and was nothing but loyal to yo' ass. She was at the gym one day doubled over in pain while you was fucking off out of the country, and I took her to the ER. Me. That's how she knows me, nigga. Anything else concerning me, feel free to ask me, 'cus I'm right here."

The deep scowl on Money's face made Azon aware that the man was pissed, and Azon gave zero fucks. He didn't care about Money's boxing title. He'd seen the man in the ring, and Azon was confident that Money couldn't beat his ass. Money was too stunned to speak for a few seconds before turning his attention back to Gia.

"You need to tell this nigga to leave, so we can talk. You threw a lil' temper tantrum, and you got my attention. You left for what? Because I spent my birthday the way I wanted to spend it? You over here entertaining another man while I'm riding around the city looking for your ass. If I didn't love you, I'd leave yo' ass right here." Money's chest heaved up and down because he was livid. While he was at home going crazy, Gia was over here in this nigga's face.

Gia's eyes narrowed into slits. "I threw a temper tantrum? That's why I'm gone. You always try to make my feelings invalid, irrelevant, or petty. You act like you don't see what you're doing wrong and how you're hurting me. Getting your attention is what I've tried to do for the last year. I'm past that. I don't want you anymore, Money. The man for me isn't one that will make me feel like it's too much to ask of him to assure me that I'm loved, appreciated and valued."

"And this is the nigga you want?" he spat tossing a disgusted look in Azon's direction.

Azon chuckled angrily and flicked the tip of his nose. "You got 'bout one more time to reference me like you know me and as if I'm not standing here, bitch." Azon's tone was low but laced with ice.

"Bitch?" Money repeated with his eyes narrowed. "Nigga, you got me fucked up."

Azon started towards Money and forgetting all about the soreness in her body, Gia jumped in front of Azon and placed her hand on his chest. "Please," she begged with her words and her eyes. "Please no."

Money was offended. He didn't feel that Gia jumped in front of that nigga because she feared what Money would do to him. She was trying to protect that nigga like she gave a fuck about him. Like he was somehow a threat to Money. Azon's orbs left Money's contorted face and landed on Gia's concerned one.

"Only for you, but he better shut the fuck up talking to me and you."

Money kissed his teeth. "Fucking wow. All the money and time I wasted on your muhfuckin' ass. Yeah, you belong in the streets." Money seethed as he stalked back towards his vehicle while Azon laughed.

"How much bread you spend? I'll give you that shit back tonight. Give me a number."

Money ignored him and kept walking. Once he was in his car, Gia breathed a sigh of relief. "I am so sorry."

Azon's brows furrowed. "What are you sorry for? You can't control that lame ass nigga's actions. I have to get up early in the morning, so I'm gonna head out. Get some rest," he peered into her eyes seemingly concerned about her and unbothered behind Money.

Gia gave him a small smile. "I will. Be careful getting home. You still look like you feel good," she teased.

"If you wanted me to sober up, you would've let me beat the fuck out that nigga," he smirked making Gia slap his chest lightly.

"Goodnight, Azon."

"Goodnight, baby."

He didn't miss the way him calling her baby made her body tremble. Yeah, he was gon' have fun getting at her and pissing Money's lame ass off in the process.

Nine

With each blow Azon delivered to the gloves that Islande was wearing a deep grunt left his body. A former boxer by the name of Cleo stood back and analyzed Azon's moves like he did every time the kid came into the gym. He observed Azon's weaknesses and his strengths. His timing could improve just a smidge, and his footwork could use some practice, but his jabs were powerful, and his hand work was amazing. Cleo had been watching Azon for more than fifteen minutes before the man took off his head gear and peeled his gloves off. He was dripping in sweat and breathing hard after his intense workout. The sport of boxing was a strenuous one indeed, but Cleo was willing to bet money the man smoked weed. His timing and stamina could definitely improve if he gave that vice up.

Cleo climbed over the ropes and stepped into the ring prompting Azon and Islande to focus their attention on him.

"My name is Cleo. This is the third time I've seen you come in here and spar. You ever thought about doing paid boxing matches?"

The question wasn't an offensive one, but Azon frowned a bit. It was a question he'd heard many times before, and his response would be the same one that he'd given just as many times. "Nah. This is just some shit I do for fun. I'm not even trying to be spending half my days in the gym working like crazy to be offered a few thousand dollars for a fight. I'm good on that. I'd rather do it for free and for fun."

"What if I can offer you $10,000 to fight one of Diamond Cove's best boxers?"

That got Azon's attention but not for the amount of money that was specified. He wasn't that rich that he'd turn down $10,000 without thinking about it. The only other time that he'd been offered to be paid for a fight was a few years back. He had been offered $1,500 *if* he won, and Azon laughed in the man's face. He was well aware that he had skills but to fight with people watching him, Azon knew he'd have to stop treating boxing like a hobby and really train for it. If he was focused on boxing, he couldn't make money like he normally did and if he had to abandon making money, he damn sure needed to be compensated more than $1,500.

But $10,000 he could work with for sure. He could make $10,000 in a week hustling, but Azon was determined to do both. Especially if it meant beating Money's ass. That was one of the most appealing things Azon had ever been offered. He wanted to beat the man's ass for free, so this would be a win win.

"Who is Diamond Cove's best boxer?" he played dumb.

"Money. He's only lost one match of his career, and he's won 22."

"That's what's up," Azon gave a brief head nod. "When would I be fighting him?"

Azon didn't miss the gleam in Cleo's eyes. It was obvious that this man could no longer box and wanted to live vicariously and make a few dollars off the next young and upcoming boxer. "He has a fight coming up in four weeks. Of course, he has to rest and have time to train after that fight, so I'd say we can set something up for seven weeks if he agrees."

Losing to Money didn't even cross his mind. Of course, it was possible, but Azon wasn't worried. At all. "Set it up then. What we gotta do?"

"If this is the only fight that you want to participate in, we can draw up a contract with me acting as the event organizer, but I'm interested in being your manager. As an amateur boxer, I can't promise you I can get you $10,000 for every fight, but I can at least get you $5,000. If you can book six fights a year, that's $30,000. That might not be a lot of money, but the longer you stay with it and the better you get, you may be able to bring in bigger crowds, get more money, and endorsement deals."

Azon nodded his understanding. Thirty thousand in one year wasn't a lot of money. But if he had the money coming in from boxing, when he did want to pay off a car, get a house, etc. he'd have legit income that he could use. He might also be able to wash some of his drug money through boxing. Azon was already thinking of opening up a gym of his own and giving kids boxing lessons. The wheels were turning in his head as Cleo spoke.

"I also understand that you can't live off $30,000 a year, so if you have other things going on that's your business. For this particular fight, I'd want to start your training next week. No weed, no alcohol, no junk food, and five days a week for two hours a day we do HITT training, mitt work, sparring, or boxing drills depending on the day. Two weeks before the fight, we up training to six days a week four hours a day."

Azon almost told Cleo's ass never mind at the mention of no weed. Azon was focused, but he was focused on fast money. Why go through all this hell when he could make way more, smoking, eating bad, drinking, and only working out when he wanted to. Azon had to force himself to look at the bigger picture. And as much as he would enjoy knocking Money out, that wasn't even the bigger picture to him. Having something legal that he could brag to his parents about was the bigger picture. The $10,000 that Azon made from the fight could go straight to a savings account and from then on, any money that he made from boxing wouldn't be touched until he was ready to buy a house or some shit. Thirty thousand dollars would be a nice start for a down payment on a house.

"Count me in," Azon responded making Cleo's day while secretly hoping he wasn't biting off more than he could chew.

***

Gia was shocked to look up and see her father entering her boutique. They hadn't spoken since she left his house a week ago. Gia almost wondered if he was coming to apologize, but the frown lines creasing his forehead told her that he was pissed about something.

"I need to talk to you," he stated a little too aggressively for her liking. She had customers and two other employees working, and he would not come to her place of business and chastise her like she was a child.

"We can step into my office," she replied with raised brows. She wasn't sure what had her father on ten, but she wasn't in the mood to be lectured. Gia didn't care if Money's boxing game was off. He'd better man up and get the fuck over it the same way she had to.

Gia led her father to the back of the store where her office was located. The smell of vanilla met her as she walked inside and made her way to the chair behind her desk. Gia was dressed in a simple black sundress and silver, sparkly, slides. She crossed her legs and peered at her father.

"Who is this lil' nigga that you've been running around with?"

"Excuse me?" Gia drew back. The way her father was coming at her it would be hard to believe that she was a grown ass twenty-five-year-old woman. This was the same way he'd come at her about Money, and Gia was growing quite tired of explaining herself.

"Money told me that you had some nigga named Azon at his house. He then caught you with the same nigga a few nights ago at Havanna's house, and now Cleo is reaching out to Money and me about Money fighting this nigga for $10,000. The most Money has ever been offered for a fight is $15,000, and he's more than twenty fights in. So who is this person that no one has ever heard of that's getting ten racks to fight Money even though that number is beneath Money, it's damn near an unheard of number for an unheard of boxer. I told Money not to even waste his time, but he feels like engaging in a dick swinging contest over pride."

Gia clicked her tongue. "First off, respectfully, I am grown. What I do is my business. I am single, and I'm no longer with Money. He didn't catch me doing anything. He popped up at Havanna's, and I was sitting in my friend's car. As far as Azon being at Money's home, he wasn't even there for ten minutes. He lifted the boxes that I couldn't because of my surgery, and he took them to my car. He's a friend. I've never even been out on a date with him, and I'm not sleeping with him. So, I don't see how getting him to move five boxes from my ex's home was disrespectful to Money."

"It's a problem because the nigga came crying to me about it. Money is going to let this bullshit drama ruin his career. How is that going to look you all of a sudden dating a new man that just so happens to want to hop in the ring with Money? You don't think this nigga is using you for clout? You have to earn a match with a boxer like Money not hang out with his ex for it. This shit is all kinds of fucked up."

Gia could practically see steam coming from her father's ears, and the angrier he got, the more pissed she became. "You're in here barking on me like I've done something wrong, and I don't appreciate it. Okay you told me so. You told me not to date Money, and we ended up not working out two years later. It's my fault. I should have listened. But you can't sit here and blame me for something that I have no control over. How is Azon using me for clout, when he doesn't even have an interest in boxing for real? He does it for fun. I've been in the gym, and I've seen him spar and when he does spar, everyone in the gym stops and stares. Cleo would have never come to you about a match if he didn't think Azon was worthy. I'm sure he reached out to Azon and not the other way around."

Gia knew that her father was smart enough to know that Cleo wouldn't be trying to put together a bullshit fight. They could pop that shit that $10,000 was beneath Money, but Money wasn't rich off fights. He was comfortable off fights, endorsements, and social media. He got around $4,500 a month from Facebook, Instagram, and Tik Tok combined from doing reels and going live. He had a few paid endorsements with different companies and the biggest one he'd received thus far was $35,000 to work with a clothing brand for nine months. If it wasn't for those things, Money would be somewhere working a 9-5 when he wasn't boxing. Blake was trying to get him in the big leagues, but that would take time.

Money accepting $10,000 for a fight wouldn't be the dumbest thing in the world. It would be almost like free money if he was as confident in his skills as he pretended to be. He was threatened by Azon, and Gia could see that with her eyes closed. His worst fear would be losing that fight to Azon and looking stupid in front of everyone especially when his ex was entertaining the nigga. Gia wasn't even officially dating Azon, and she hated that she was already being dragged into drama. She fought for her relationship, and it didn't work. Why should she have to be punished? So because Azon boxed, she couldn't hang out with him? Who in the hell made that dumb ass rule?

Blake pushed out a deep breath. "I'm begging you. If you ever cared about Money at all end this shit until this next fight. Go apologize, talk to him, stroke his ego if you have to. Do whatever you have to do to put his head in the game and most of all that includes leaving that Azon nigga alone."

The shock that she felt from his words almost made her mouth fall open. But rather than her mouth falling open, it turned down. The disappointment on her face was evident to anyone that cared but Gia was learning that much like Money, her father didn't really give a damn about what made her happy.

"No," she answered calmly. "I have done nothing wrong, and I will not apologize. He didn't want the relationship enough to work for it, so why does he care that I left? He should be happy that I'm not there nagging him and stressing him out. I will not kiss his ass, so he can win some lame ass fight."

Gia's stomach felt heavy as Blake's eyes widened. "Were the fights lame when you were defying me to be with his ass and at every match cheering him on? Were the fights lame when you left my home to go live in the house that his fights were paying for?"

Gia pinched the bridge of her nose. She couldn't believe the way her father was stressing her out. All that mattered to him was Money winning his fight. He couldn't care less how Gia felt, and that shit hurt, but she was going to take it to the chin like she did everything else.

"I will never disrespect you, so I have nothing else to say on the matter. I'm not a child, and you can't keep talking to me like one because you care more about the income that Money brings you more than my feelings." Gia held her head high and stuck her chin out as she tried to appear confident but really, she wanted to cry. Same shit different day.

Blake's red face told Gia all that she needed to know. Her father was livid, but she really didn't care. She wasn't kissing Money's ass, so he could win a fight, and she wasn't going to stop talking to Azon to stroke Money's ego. Had he done what she requested many times and made her feel loved in their relationship, Azon could never have come in and gotten as far as he had. Yes, he was charming, handsome, and charismatic, but Gia prided herself on being faithful. If Money was doing his job, and she was truly happy, she would've never needed Azon to move her boxes, and she would have never been caught sitting in his car outside of Havanna's home.

Rather than Blake talking to Money one grown man to another and telling him that he dropped the ball and had to deal with the consequences, her father was blaming her. That was some sick shit. It made Gia appreciate Azon that much more. Yes, all men appeared to be heaven sent in the beginning, but she didn't believe his manners and his respect were fake. Something about the way he spoke to her, looked at her, and handled her, let Gia know that he'd never make her feel less than. He'd never make her question what she meant to him, and he'd never make her feel wrong for doing what was right for her. That was some shit her own father wasn't even doing at the moment.

"We don't have anything else to talk about. I hope you know what you're doing." Blake stood up. "If you want to appear to be some kind of disloyal boxing groupie, then there isn't anything I can do about it. Just know that when that lil' Azon nigga hurts your feelings, there won't be a thing I can do."

Gia cocked her head to the side. "Why do you think I'd expect you to do anything? You hurt my feelings all the time and don't seem to care. You're mad at me right now because Money has been hurting my feelings for years, but I shouldn't have broken up with him before a fight. You have made it abundantly clear that you don't care about my feelings at all. So, if I had problems with anyone else, I can assure you that I'd never come to you."

Blake's upper lip curled into a snarl and a look of such disdain from her own father made tears fill Gia's eyes as soon as her father turned his back. This was a fine ass mess that she'd managed to get herself into.

Ten

Two days later, Gia sat across from Azon in a dimly lit restaurant taking in his handsome features. Even with his thick wicks, he didn't seem out of place at all in the posh restaurant. He was dressed in khaki pants, a Gucci shirt, and wheat-colored Timbs. His cologne left a trail behind him when he walked, and he had a crisp line up that gave him zaddy vibes. Gia was dressed in white, linen shorts, a white camisole, a green blazer, and gold strappy Tom Ford heels. Her braids were hanging freely, and she'd opted to wear light make-up for the occasion. This was the most done up that Azon had ever seen her and though she was fine as hell with a bare face, with make-up on, she gave baddie for sure.

"You have something you want to tell me?" she asked before picking up her glass and sipping her wine.

"Yeah, I do." Azon sat up straight and licked his lips. "I'm honored to be here with you tonight. I know you just wasted a lot of time with a fuck nigga, and I expect you to be a little closed off and guarded. It's cool. I don't mind working for what I want though."

Gia was drinking the good stuff, and three large sips had her body feeling warm. She was also loose and a little less reserved. After giggling at his comment, she took another sip before placing the glass back down. "Flattery will get you everywhere, but that's not what I mean, and you know it. Are you trying to fight Money in a boxing match?"

Azon's brows lifted. "That nigga told you that?"

"No, he went crying to my father. Cleo one of my father's unspoken rivals also reached out to him. My father is pissed that as a more well-known boxer, Money is being offered such a low amount of money. He feels it's an insult but at the same time, he wants to know how someone unknown was offered so much."

Azon chuckled. "No disrespect, babe, but your pops is worried about the wrong shit. Me and what I get offered is none of his concern." Azon picked up his glass of cognac and drank some. "And if it's such a lowball offer that's beneath him, why doesn't he just say no and keep it pushing? Why all the extra shit?"

Gia pushed out a small sigh. "Money is so threatened by you it's not even funny. He probably went to my father crying real tears. And it gets better. He told my father that I had you at his house, and he caught me sitting in the car with you. My father basically called me a groupie for boxers, and he's damn near ready to disown me because I won't apologize to Money. His head is all fucked up, and if he loses his next fight, it'll be my fault."

Azon drew back with narrowed eyes. "Yo what the fuck kind of man is your pops? That shit about to piss me off for real." Gia could tell by the way he was clenching his back teeth together that he was angry, and that warmed her heart. Azon made her believe that he'd go to war with a hundred niggas behind her. "I'd never just disrespect your people but that's lame as hell. How are you a groupie for boxers, and I'm not even a boxer? I'm just a talented ass nigga that could dust Money's ass and people see that shit."

Gia shook her head. "It's a mess. My father is a great provider. He made it early in life. He and my mom got married when they were twenty-three and less than two years later, he had her living in a gated community. He has always taken care of my mom, and he loves her. He loves me and my sister, but he just isn't the best with expressing himself. Everything has to be that tough love bullshit. He acts like it will kill him to be soft with me and my sister. He never wanted me to date Money because he didn't want me to get hurt and because Money was in his prime. He knew that it would be easy for Money to get distracted and fuck up his career. He forbade me to date Money, and I was grown as fuck."

Azon shook his head and finished off his drink.

"When he found out that Money and I were still sneaking around dating each other, we got into it bad, and I moved out and went to live with Money. We eventually got over it, but he's always made it clear that he doesn't care what happens, his main concern is Money's career. Money could probably send me home to that man with a black eye, and he wouldn't care because he told me not to date Money."

A deep scowl appeared on Azon's face. "That's some sucka ass shit. No wonder you fell for a lame like Money. You're related to a sucka ass nigga."

Gia didn't even take offense to Azon talking about her father, and that surprised her. Gia could have a knock down drag out fight with anyone in her family, and she would talk cash shit about them, but that didn't mean a stranger could. Azon wasn't saying anything wrong about her father though, and she wasn't about to stop him. Seeing him angry at the way her father was treating her made her warmer than the wine did. Gia went back to drinking, and the waitress brought their food over to the table.

"So, I don't think the fight with you and Money will happen. He's going to blame it on the money, but I know the truth. Are you going to look into fighting someone else?" Gia ate some of her Singapore noodles.

"I'm not sure. Cleo wants me to fight Money bad as hell, and that's why he offered me such a high amount. I have a feeling if I fight a lesser known boxer that the amount will decline. I never wanted to take boxing serious because it takes so much time and dedication, and I have other things I could be doing that will put more money in my pocket for less work."

Gia figured that Azon sold drugs, but she didn't feel like it was an appropriate question to ask and in a way, she didn't want to know. Maybe that was naïve of her, but she felt ignorance was bliss. She didn't hold a personal vendetta against drug dealers, but she knew the dangers that were associated with that life. Maybe he wasn't a drug dealer. He could have been a robber or a killer, but with her, he was a sexy ass gentleman, and that's all she cared to know. Money didn't do anything illegal except smoke weed sometimes, and if Azon was a criminal, it didn't negate the fact that he treated her better than Money ever had. And that was sad seeing as how she hadn't even known Azon for that long versus knowing Money for more than two years.

"I think you should look into it. I can't tell you what to do, but it's safe in the sense that you can make honest money off it. And I hope that doesn't sound like I'm judging you because I don't know that you don't already make honest money. But you are so talented. Anyone with eyes that knows the sport of boxing can see that. Who taught you how to box?"

"Our next door neighbor used to babysit us sometimes when our parents were at work, and her boyfriend taught me and Islande to box. I picked up on it faster and liked it more than Islande did, so he talked my pops into getting me lessons which said something because my father doesn't believe in wasting money. He did though, and I took lessons for three years."

"Well, whoever taught you is the truth. I really feel like you can go far, and don't just think about what you can get from actual fights. You can charge others for boxing lessons. You can get brand deals and endorsements. You can become an entire brand."

"I had already been thinking about that. I was actually thinking of opening a gym. Safe money is definitely the goal for my future. I've been thinking about that a lot lately."

"For real? You never really thought about it before?"

Azon shrugged passively. "Not really. I'm a day to day type nigga. I don't have certain goals like I want to buy a crib by the age of thirty. I just know I don't want to be broke, and I want some shit out of life. I didn't really put end date on it. What about you? What are your plans for the future?"

"They have definitely changed." Gia chuckled. "I think within the next year, I want to have a second stream of income. I'm not sure what that is yet, and for my birthday next year, I want to buy a house. That's really it for now. I saw myself being married with kids in the next five years but..." her voice trailed off, and she picked up her glass of wine and finished it off.

The waitress came and refilled their glasses. Azon said thank you and responded to Gia. "I know things can change in the blink of an eye for sure, but I think I'll become more intentional about goals. Maybe meeting them and crossing them off my list will give me a sense of feeling accomplished, and I'll start to do it more."

Gia smiled wide. "I think that's a great idea."

"As far as that second stream of income goes, you can be my personal cheerleader," he smirked flirtatiously making her laugh.

"And how much does that pay?"

"Enough."

She laughed harder. Gia had been sulking for the past few days over her conversation with her father, but being in Azon's presence was making her feel so much better. His charm made her feel full. He wasn't the type of man to work sex into every conversation. He wasn't touchy feely with her right out the gate, and he could engage in meaningful conversation. All of those were points in his favor. The pair ordered dessert and before they knew it, dinner was over.

There was a sinking feeling in the pit of Gia's stomach. She wasn't ready for their night to be over. She wasn't sure if she should express that and risk coming off a bit thirsty, or just relax and be on whatever type of time Azon was on. She led the way to the door, but he was right behind her with his hand on the small of her back. When they reached her car, Gia turned around to face him, and he was so much in her personal space that their noses were almost touching.

"I had fun with you tonight." Azon tugged at the bottom of her blazer. "Drive safely."

Gia swallowed hard because it was now or never. The thought of him turning to walk away made her care less about being presumptuous. "What if I don't want the fun to end?"

A smirk stretched across Azon's lips. "Oh word? What you want to do?"

Gia simpered. "I don't know. Something corny like sit on the beach and talk. I love sitting on the beach at night."

Azon gripped her chin lightly, and her breath hitched in her throat as he peered into her eyes. "We can do that. We can stop at one of those little stores on the strip and get some towels to sit on. As a matter of fact, just follow me to my house. We can get towels from there, and you can leave your car parked there."

Gia nodded. Inside her car, her teeth sank into her bottom lip, and a smile managed to peek through. Being with Azon was exciting. Maybe she looked bad to Money and her father for moving on so quickly, but Gia was trying her hardest not to care. If doing what made her feel good made them feel some kind of way then so be it. She wasn't responsible for their feelings. Gia was going to start being just as selfish as they were. Only caring about herself and what made her happy and at the moment, it was Azon. She was going to take a page from his book and not think too deep into it. No plans of a future with him. Just one day at a time.

Gia trailed Azon's car into a pretty nice neighborhood. He pulled up in the driveway, and she parked beside his car. While she waited on him to retrieve the towels, Gia, popped some gum into her mouth and refreshed her lip gloss. When she saw him walking back to the car with two fluffy towels in one hand and his other hand caressing his dick, she smiled. Gia got out of the car as Azon walked around to the passenger side of his car and held the door open for her.

"Thank you," she smiled as she eased past him and into his car. The car was so clean you could eat off the floor, and the air fresheners in the car gave it a masculine smell. Gia's brow lifted at the subtle sounds of Jazmine Sullivan playing from the car's speakers, and that turned her on. She half expected Azon to be blasting some shoot 'em up bang bang type of trap or drill music. It seemed to be a reoccurring thing for him to surprise her, and Gia loved that about him.

Azon placed the towels in the backseat and put his gear in reverse. His phone was vibrating, and the screen was lighting up in his lap, but Azon ignored each call as he maneuvered his car down the street.

"Have you only ever lived in Florida and North Carolina?" she inquired. Maybe she wasn't going to marry him, but if she was going to be hanging out with him and being all hot and bothered by his alluring presence, she wanted to know more about him.

"Nah. I lived in Haiti up until I was four. From there we went to Florida. What about you?" he looked over at her.

"Unfortunately, I've only ever lived here. I mean don't get me wrong, I like North Carolina but before I opened my boutique and got into a relationship, I told myself I'd be something like a nomad for two or three years. I wanted to just live in different places for a bit and experience the food, the culture, the change of scenery. Hawaii, New Orleans, and the mountains were on my list."

"That sounds kind of dope. I could see me doing some shit like that."

Gia wasn't sure why, but she smiled. That would be a heck of an adventure. Gia was sure she'd follow his sexy ass anywhere he went. With a subtle shake of her head, she turned and stared out of the window. Inwardly, she reminded herself to reel it back in. He said he could see himself doing some shit like that. He didn't say he would actually do it or that he would do it with her. *No plans and no goals.* Gia was determined to learn how to just have fun and not think so deep into things. By her second date with Money, she was wondering what their kids would look like, and that was her problem. She fell too soon and too hard for potential. She was going to stop doing that.

Jazmine Sullivan went off, and Jhene Aiko began to play. "You like R&B, huh?" she asked.

"I like all kinds of music. I'll even listen to some country shit for real. My playlist is complex as fuck. Music makes me happy. Certain songs bring back the craziest memories for me be it from childhood, my first time getting pussy, or my first time hitting a lick. I even remember the song that was playing the first time I got in a boxing ring. I don't have to hear that gangsta shit all day every day. I really live that shit."

Gia squeezed her thighs together. *Down girl,* she hoped her pussy could hear her inner thoughts. At that point, Azon probably could have told her that he turned into a werewolf when there was a full moon, and she probably wouldn't have cared. At the beach, Azon parked, and they got out of the car. Gia removed her heels and walked barefoot beside Azon. It was dark out, so there weren't many people there, but a few people would walk by here and there. Azon found a spot and placed the towels side by side.

"Security be out here and shit?" he looked around. "I'm trying to smoke my blunt."

"I don't think they're out here this late." There were a few times after getting into an argument with Money that Gia would come sit by the water late at night. She'd listen to the waves crash against the shore for hours while being lost in her thoughts. She rarely ever saw security out after a certain time. Azon lit a blunt that was already rolled, and the pungent aroma wafted into her nostrils.

Gia didn't smoke, but the weed he was inhaling into his lungs smelled good as hell, and she hoped for a slight contact high. "I told my brother where I was and who I was with just in case you get any ideas. If I don't make it back home safe with my clothes intact, he gon' be looking for your ass," Azon joked making her laugh.

"Clothes intact? You think I'm gon' rape you?"

"You might. Sexy as I am. I be having to beat 'em off with a stick."

Gia giggled louder. "I promise I'll try to keep my composure."

"Seriously though, it's good to see you smiling and having fun. Don't let your father's ignorant ass opinions or a break-up with a lame steal your joy."

She turned to look at Azon, who was staring out at the ocean. With a smile on her face, she studied the side of his face as he pulled from the blunt. "You can't ever reference Money without calling him lame or corny."

Azon shrugged passively. "Am I lying though?"

Gia chose not to answer. She just snuggled up next to Azon and laid her head on his shoulder. Maybe she was doing too much too fast, but she was doing what felt natural to her. Her promise about keeping her composure had gone out the window just that fast. Azon made her feel safe. She was comfortable enough to let her guard down with him. He continued smoking, and no words were spoken between the two of them until he finished his blunt, turned his head to the side, and kissed her forehead.

"You good?" he asked in a low tone that sent chills down her spine.

Gia lifted her head and boldly placed her mouth on his. One peck that lingered for a few seconds turned into him parting her lips with his tongue and kissing her deeply. Azon tongued her down like he'd been waiting for that moment all his life. He placed one hand around her neck and choked her lightly while they kissed as a puddle formed in her panties. Azon moved down to her neck and sucked on her flesh hungrily. A moan escaped her lips as he moved down to her breasts. Gripping one of her C cups in his hand, he gently bit her nipple before flickering his tongue over it, then taking it into his mouth.

Gia grabbed a handful of his wicks as she bit her bottom lip and enjoyed the feel of his mouth on her body. Azon placed a trail of wet kisses from her breast to her belly button. Before she knew it, she was out of her shorts and panties and laid back on the towel while his head was buried in between her thighs. Gia's back arched, and she caressed the back of his head while slightly lifting her hips and feeding herself to him. Azon moaned into her honeypot, and moans filled the air as Gia rode his face. His lips locked around her pearl, and he sucked her into an orgasm that made her toes curl.

Gia's body went limp as Azon feasted on her sweetness. When he was satisfied, he moved over and started sucking on the inside of her thigh. Gia's head was reeling. The sucking stopped, and she heard the sound of a condom wrapper being ripped open. There was some fidgeting, and then he was entering her. Gia's ballerina shaped nails dug into Azon's back while she bit the inside of her cheek as she adjusted to his size.

"Ummmm," she moaned slightly wondering if all of him would fit inside her.

"Si bon," he whispered in her ear, and she had no idea what it even meant, but her body relaxed, and she opened up wider for the sexy bilingual man that had her head spinning at the moment. She was so lost in Azon that she was having sex out in the open.

Azon groaned as he pushed further and deeper. Gia's snugness was sucking him in. Since she refreshed his memory on how sensual and erotic kissing could be, he snaked his tongue back into her mouth while he grinded into her middle. Not even caring about the fact that she was outside, Gia closed her eyes and enjoyed every moment that was Azon. His manhood felt as if it had been designed specifically for her walls. The deeper he kissed her and the more savagely he stroked her, the wetter she became. When he moved his mouth over to her ear and said God only knows what to her in French, her body trembled as her stomach spasmed, and a tornado of an orgasm ripped through her body.

Havanna had joked with her many times that if she found the man that could make her cum from penetration alone, she'd be crazy over his ass, and Gia could tell already that she hadn't lied. Azon checked every single last box that a woman could have on her list for a man.

"Damn you wet this dick up," Azon breathed before he gently bit her neck and released into the condom with a grunt.

The pair basked in the highs from their orgasms for all of two seconds before Azon pulled out of her. As he stood up, they heard a child playing and shrieking in the distance, and Gia jumped up like her ass was on fire. They could tell that the child was a good distance away from them, but it had reminded them that they were having sex outside. Gia giggled lightly as she rushed to get dressed. She was glad it was dark, so Azon couldn't see her biting her bottom lip and blushing. The smile that was on her face wouldn't leave despite the fact that they could have been caught by people walking by.

Azon picked the towels up and shook the sand from them. He then pulled Gia into him and peered into her eyes with one hand wrapped around her waist. "You good?"

It was something that he asked her often, and each time he asked it made her smile.

"Yes. I'm good, Azon."

He pecked her lips before grabbing her hand and walking her to the car.

Eleven

"If you're not going to Sunday dinner then I'm not either because daddy has been in a piss poor mood, and I don't want to hear the shit," Kaylin frowned. Gia and her sister had met up for lunch because they hadn't seen each other since Gia left her parents' house to go stay with Havanna.

Gia frowned too before sipping her strawberry lemonade. "Heck no, I'm not going over there. I'm probably not even welcomed at his dinner table," she rolled her eyes upwards. The way Blake had his ass on his back about Money and this upcoming fight plus the fight he'd been offered against Azon was insane.

Kaylin snickered. "Mommy said she overheard daddy yelling at Money last night telling him he needed to stop acting like a bitch."

Gia shook her head. "It's nice to see that I'm not the only one that daddy doesn't give a damn about. He couldn't care less about Money. All daddy cares about is if he can get Money to the big leagues what it will mean to his bank account."

"You know daddy loves you, but when it comes to boxing, he's a different kind of beast. You know mommy almost left him back in the day for about the same reason you left Money. Only difference is, daddy got his act together. But that man lives, breathes, eats, and shits boxing. Since he can't do it anymore, he has to be around it any way that he can and that's Money at the moment. I know he's also pissed that Cleo got his hands on Azon before he could discover him. You know daddy has been talking about new talent for a moment."

"And while he wants me to kiss Money's ass, he needs to think about what that will mean for him. Because I heard Money's spoiled ass distinctly tell him that he didn't want him representing anyone else."

"How in the hell does he think he can tell another man how many people he can manage?"

"I'm telling you. With every fight that he won, Money's ego got bigger and bigger. That man walked around with his head in the clouds like he was making millions."

"Well, he's trying to act like he's too good to fight Azon, but everyone else is saying it's fear. Damn near the whole city is talking about this fight, and no one even knows who this Azon character is. Wait a minute, let me correct that. Most of us don't know who he is, but I heard you do," she smirked, and Gia threw a balled-up napkin at her.

Gia kissed her teeth while Kaylin giggled. "Your daddy talks too much."

"Baby, I got this tea from mommy. I'm glad I didn't get it from daddy because as soon as I would have told him you aren't doing anything wrong, he would have fussed me out about some shit I did last year. That man is crazy. Money fumbled you, and you can date who you want. I don't care if it's another boxer or the boxer's damn daddy." When it came to the sisters, they stuck together anytime Blake got on that bullshit and chastised them over stupid things. Sometimes, he'd get so angry at them defending one another that he'd curse both of them out.

Gia shrugged passively in an effort to try and downplay her attraction to Azon. Truth was, she woke up thinking about the man, and she hated that for herself. Gia had no plans to go from having feelings for one man straight to another. She needed time to focus, get her head right, then get back in the game. She never wanted to be that woman that didn't feel complete unless she had a man. That's not a type of co-dependency that she ever wanted for herself.

"I kept seeing Azon around town. He literally came in the gym one time when I was there with Money, then I saw him again at the fight, and again at the racetrack. He was also at the gym the day my appendix ruptured, and he took me to the ER. I guess I should add that he came in the boutique after I saw him at the racetrack, and he was flirting with me, but I told him I had a man. He left it at that. But at the ER when he found out me and Money broke up, he asked me out. Daddy is making it seem like I was hanging out every day at the gym trying to throw pussy at any nigga with boxing gloves on," Gia kissed her teeth in annoyance.

Kaylin waved the comment off. "The last thing I would do is get in my feelings behind daddy. Yes, we love him, but we're grown as hell, and he be tripping. You've had two boyfriends in your entire life, and one of them barely counts because it was some high school shit. The fact that he even referenced you as a groupie was distasteful as shit. Again, the man has issues. Don't make his issues yours. Ignore his ass like me and mommy do."

Gia nodded, but it was easier said than done. Blake bought her first car. He supported her dreams of opening a boutique. He was her first hero. She was already a daddy's girl when she hit her teenage years and the tough love and insensitivity reared its' ugly head. Gia began to hate her father's brashness, but she still loved him as her provider and protector. She didn't like when they were on the outs and not speaking, but she refused to let him talk to her crazy and try to dictate her moves when she was very much an adult.

The sisters ended their meal and parted ways. As she was buckling her seatbelt, Gia got a text from Azon inviting her over to his house later. He stated that he was cooking, and he wanted her to taste his food.

'That's not all I want to taste.'

Gia relaxed in her leather seat as impure thoughts flooded her brain. With a small simper, she texted him back and told him she'd love to come over. He gave her a time and an address and after checking her watch, Gia saw that she had time to stop by her boutique. She was pleasantly surprised at the smooth way things had run while she was out. Her employees didn't let her down and as a token of her appreciation, Gia was going to do something nice for them. She thought about adding an extra $300 in everyone's check. She wasn't rich, but she didn't have a lot of employees, so it would be feasible. She almost worried that $300 wasn't enough but while she was away, all they'd done was their jobs. Most people wouldn't have rewarded them for that, but Gia wanted to make them feel appreciated.

When she walked into the boutique, she smiled widely at Ajonique and Khris. They were behind the register talking, and when Gia appeared they jumped slightly as if she'd caught them doing something wrong. Gia's brows lifted as she wondered why they were looking like deer caught in headlights. If there were customers in the boutique, Gia wanted them to walk around and be ready to help the customer at any given time as well as make sure no one was stealing. Gia was a small business, and thieves would end her if she let them. She couldn't afford to take tons of losses on stolen merchandise.

She also didn't care if they checked a text message every now and again, but Gia didn't want them standing where customers could see them engrossed in their phones and looking unprofessional. Ninety-nine percent of the time, they should be straightening clothes, engaging with customers, answering emails, and fulfilling online orders. There shouldn't be a lot of time to stand around and talk, but Gia walked a fine line between lenient boss, and the *I'm not your friend,* kind of boss.

Her eyes narrowed as she walked towards the women, and their orbs were dancing nervously around the room. Any other time, they were happy to see her, running up on her, offering compliments, and telling her about crazy or rude customers. Today, they were both acting off, and she wanted to know why.

"What's up with y'all?" she stood in front of the counter that they were behind. She looked down and saw Khris's phone on the counter, and the page was open to an Instagram blog site. "Oh you got caught on social media when you should be working?" Gia's brows hiked up. She'd caught all of her employees doing wrong things before, and they never looked like they'd swallowed a bumble bee. Eyes wide, strained looks on their faces. They were being weird indeed.

"We weren't up there like that. There aren't any customers, and Ajonique just showed me something. We weren't gossiping. I swear. We just wondered if you knew." Ajonique's throat bounced as she swallowed hard while Gia's pulse raced.

If they had seen some shit on the blogs, that could only mean that Money was involved. He was far from an A-list celebrity, but he had 245,000 followers on Instagram and a few endorsement deals, so on slow news days, blogs would report on people like him. During their two year relationship, Gia had only ended up in the blogs with him once, and that was when he lost the fight. She was glad that he wasn't more famous than he was because she had no desire for her every move to be gossip for the masses to discuss. Some females lived for that shit, but not Gia. The only good thing about him being in the blog that day was that a lot of people went to her page to see who she was and from there, her boutique got 500 orders in one day. Gia was elated but at the same time, if she could only get 500 orders by being in a blog, she'd rather not. Going viral to chase clout and money wasn't her cup of tea unless she was going viral for something good.

Before Gia could respond, she looked at her phone that was pinging back-to-back and saw that she had 45 new orders for her boutique. Pushing out a small sigh coupled with a groan she mumbled, "What is it? Might as well let me see." Her brows were furrowed already because she knew this was about to be some bullshit.

With a sheepish expression on her face, Khris picked the phone up and passed it to Gia. Gia's breath caught in her throat as she saw some either super light-skinned or white chick in a hotel room getting dressed with Money in the background talking on the phone. Gia's eyes narrowed into slits as she observed the hotel room. Something in her gut told her that it wasn't an

American hotel room. She turned the volume up and listened to the woman with too big veneers speak. She had been on Instagram live at the time, and someone had screen recorded it. She was probably a nobody just like Gia and since Money was a slight nobody, it took the blogs a few days to get the tea. But they had it now. Light bright damn near white squinted her eyes as she read the comments coming on her screen.

"Yeah, we're in London. About to go get something to eat. His friends came too, so after we do dinner, we're going to a club. Y'all I didn't know clubs in London be lit like this. We had so much fun last night."

Gia's body temperature rose as her chest tightened. Embarrassing ass fuck ass nigga. She wanted to cry but not from sadness. From anger. She knew it. She already knew the shit, but that didn't mean she wanted to see it. Just when she thought she was done crying. Just when she thought she was moving past her heartbreak, something had to rear its' ugly head and let her know that there was more bullshit needing her attention.

Doesn't he have a girlfriend?

Yeah, his girlfriend is pretty, and she owns a boutique. I can't think of her name right now.

Gia read the comments as they floated across the screen. The chick with the Mr. Potato head teeth alternated between doing her make-up and looking over the comments. Of course, she only responded to the one that she wanted. She ignored all the ones about Money having a girlfriend. But why should she care when Money didn't even care? Gia's gaze drifted down to the caption that the blogs posted with the screen recording.

Amateur boxer, Kyle Monroe aka Money was reportedly in London with Instagram model Baby Cakes. Baby Cakes appeared on season three of Wildin' Out as one of the Wildin' Out girls and was rumored to have a slight fling with Nick Cannon though she managed to escape becoming pregnant by the comedian. Last we knew, Money was in a long-term relationship, but maybe he's single again. Who knows?

Gia frowned at the name Baby Cakes and passed the phone back to Khris. "No, I didn't know, but a customer just came in, so I need the two of you to make that your priority. We just got forty-five new orders, so there's no way anyone should be standing around."

Gia walked towards her office, face burning from embarrassment. She wanted to believe that her employees had been lightly chastised for not doing their jobs, but she knew she'd been short with them because she was embarrassed. They didn't know her and Money broke up, because Gia didn't put her employees in her business. They didn't know a thing about her relationship. They only saw Money when he came into the boutique. He would occasionally send her flowers or some sort of gift to the boutique that they would gush over, but Gia kept that part of her life away from her place of business. Gia placed her elbows on her desk and put her face in her hands.

She didn't have any tears left to cry, but she wanted to tear some shit up. She wanted to go to Money's home and claw his eyes out. She fucking hated him, and she hated herself for ignoring all the red flags and staying with him for as long as she did.

After a few moments of sulking, Gia inhaled a deep breath and put her big girl panties on. She checked the back office of her website and saw that she now had 100 orders for the day. Not even that could make her smile, but she was glad that nosey people stalking her page were finding items from her boutique that they liked enough to order. With her head held high, Gia went into the inventory room and found all of the items that had been ordered online. She printed the labels and packaged the orders. By the time she was done, sixty more orders had come through. Being that she was going to be moving into her own place soon, despite the circumstances that occurred, Gia had to thank God for these orders. Gia went back to the front where Ajonique was ringing up a customer, and Khris was helping a customer.

"These orders are booming. I just did a lot, and there are more coming in. I'm going to do about twenty-five more and then what I don't finish one of you can do before you close for the night."

"Okay sounds good," Ajonique smiled, and Gia returned the gesture.

She knew the girl felt sorry for her. Shit, Gia almost felt sorry for herself, but it was what it was. When she was done packing more orders, Gia took the bank bag into her office and counted the money that had been taken from the register throughout the day. After counting $1,700 she filled out a deposit slip and placed it in the bag before zipping it back up. Gia said good-bye to the girls and headed for the bank. When she left there, she saw that she had less than an hour before Azon wanted her to come over. Gia had been running around all day, and she wanted to be freshly showered before going to his place.

Gia rushed into Havanna's house and went straight to the shower. Havanna had been pulling thirteen-hour days sometimes, and she was rarely ever home. Since she was there anyway, Gia watched Kendall some, but most days, she went to Havanna's mother. Gia washed her body quickly, dried off, and put on lotion. In just her bra and panties, she stood at the foot of her bed rummaging through her clothes until she found something cute to wear. Gia pulled out black, leather shorts, a black graphic tee, and she would wear black sandals on her feet.

After she was dressed, Gia laid her baby hair and grabbed her purse. In her car, she put Azon's address in her GPS, and her estimated arrival time was ten minutes after he told her to come, so that wasn't too bad. As she drove, Gia's mind finally had time to go back to what she'd seen in the blogs, and tears filled her eyes. Which made her angry. Crying over a nigga like Money made her mad. Gia hated being emotional. She so desperately longed to be one of those people that truly didn't give a damn about anything. Gia hated passive people, but she longed to be one. To walk around seeming unfazed by everything had to bring the ultimate peace to a person's life. Gia didn't want to care. About anything. Caring got you hurt.

When she arrived at Azon's house, Gia pushed her somber thoughts to the back of her mind and got out of her vehicle. Moments after she knocked, Azon answered the door, handsome as ever in white shorts made of sweat pant material and a red tee.

"Late ass," he joked as he held the door open for her.

Gia gave him a small smile. "Sorry. It smells absolutely delicious in here though."

As soon as she crossed the threshold, he was right there. She was in his space, and he wasn't attempting to move. "How was your day?" he asked as he peered into her eyes.

"It was a day," she smiled again, and he saw the sadness in her eyes.

"What's wrong?"

"Nothing worth talking about."

Azon chose not to push. He simply nodded his understanding and grabbed her hand to lead her to the kitchen. "We have griot, poulet aux noix, rice, and cabbage."

The aroma infiltrating her nostrils was divine. Gia's stomach growled as her mouth watered for a plate. "I don't have any idea what any of that is, but it smells awesome."

"Have a seat," Azon chuckled. "Let me fix you a plate."

Gia sat down and watched as Azon moved around the room. His locs were pulled back in a ponytail, and it was the first time she'd ever seen him without his gold fronts. She hadn't known him long, but he seemed a tad bit more muscular than he was the first time she met him.

"You been training?"

"Yeah. On my own. Nothing major. I start with Cleo next week, so Sunday is my last day smoking weed until I beat Money's ass. I'm not looking forward to that shit."

Gia's stomach sank at the mention of his name. She absolutely, positively hated Money. When Azon walked towards her with her plate in his hand, he could tell that something was bothering her. There was no life in her eyes no matter how many times she gave him a fake ass smile. Azon sat the plate down on the table and pulled Gia out of her seat. Holding both of her hands, he gazed into her eyes.

"I was trying to let it slide, but what's wrong? And don't tell me that bullshit nothing." His tone was assertive, but low, and comforting. It made her want to fall into his arms and tell him everything.

"I swear it's nothing really. I just got confirmation of what I already knew. Money was in London with his friends, but he had a woman there with him too."

Azon stared at her for a moment without speaking. He knew women were emotional creatures, so he was trying to give her grace. "I know you're going to feel some type of way because you're human. But let this be the last time you come around me, sad about that nigga. Do you know who the fuck you are? I gotta take you and let you look in the mirror to remind you?"

His words made her smile because he was serious as a heart attack. Gia wished she could turn her feelings on and off, but she was going to put forth the effort to not let Money get to her. "I'm sorry."

"You don't have to apologize to me. Apologize to yourself for letting a nigga that's beneath you steal your joy. Don't ever let anybody do that. Not me, not anybody. You got that?"

Gia nodded. Azon gripped her waist. "Good."

They peered at each other for a moment, and Gia became lost in his eyes. Azon was a different type of man. He was the furthest thing from soft there was. If he got into a fight with a grizzly bear, Gia had no doubt that the bear would need help. But with her he was the complete opposite, and it wasn't game. Azon was so comfortable and confident in everything that he did there could be nothing fake or rehearsed about it.

"Now eat your food."

Gia smiled and sat down at the table. "Yes sir."

Azon picked the fork up, scooped up a forkful of rice and fed it to her. Gia's eyes fluttered closed. She wasn't sure if she should consider herself a foodie or just greedy, but she loved to eat, and she had never in life tasted rice so flavorful.

"Azon, this is so good," she marveled.

He winked at her and passed her the fork while he went to go fix his own plate. By the time he sat down across from her, Gia had tasted everything on the plate.

"Who taught you to cook?"

"Both of my parents. They can both cook. Hell, I think my dad can cook better than my mom a lil' bit. I'd never tell her that though."

"Are you and your parents close?" Gia smiled.

Azon pushed out a slight chuckle. "Not hardly. I've been deemed a bad apple since I was like twelve, but when I graduated from high school and didn't go to college or get a job, it became official in their eyes. They swear I'm always up to no good, and that I get my money by doing the devil's work."

Gia shifted in her seat. She didn't think Azon was a bad person, but she was pretty sure he made his money in a way that most parents wouldn't approve of. That wasn't unusual. "Me and my mom are pretty close. My dad and I are so off and on, I'm not sure we can ever be described as close. After how he's been acting since my break-up, I can't even predict what our relationship will be like from here on out."

"I'm big on fixing anything that's fixable when you love someone but on the other hand, I value myself. Nobody can have that shit, and when I say nobody, I mean nobody. I don't give a fuck who I have to get rid of. I'll never compromise my peace to have anyone in my life."

"I definitely agree with that. You said Sunday is your last day smoking. Did that guy agree to do the fight?"

Azon laughed at the fact that she didn't even want to speak Money's name. "Nah. He's still acting like this shit is beneath him, but you know one of the best parts of boxing is the shit talking. Cleo uploaded a lil' bullshit video of me sparring. Training hasn't even started so whatever he captured is shit I already know and that I don't take serious. He uploaded that shit and said some shit like Money knows this boy will take his ass off and hand it to 'em. People are already placing bets, and he hasn't even agreed to it. That nigga gon' get tired of looking scared, and he's going to agree. Watch." Azon stated confidently.

Gia nodded, and the conversation continued as they ate. When she was done, she leaned back in the chair and rubbed her stomach. "That was too good, and I'm full as hell. It's kind of early. You in for the night?"

"Nah. I'm gonna clean this kitchen up, have some dessert, and then hit the streets."

Gia blushed at the way he said he was going to have some dessert. "Oh yeah? What you got in here sweet?"

"You."

The lust in his eyes had her ready to say fuck this kitchen. But she stood up and walked over to the sink to help him instead. His phone vibrated on the counter, and her eyes inadvertently fell on the screen. Gia hated that she felt a surge of jealousy when she saw he had an attachment from someone named Fallon. She looked away, but her eyes had lingered for so long that Azon caught her. "Unlock it and see what she sent," he stated casually, and her head whipped in his direction.

"Huh?"

Azon chuckled. "I see you looking with your looking ass, so unlock the phone. I don't care," he shrugged passively, and her jaw slacked. In the two years, she'd been with Money he would have rather cut off his own finger than give her the passcode to his phone.

Gia didn't want to care what was in his phone. She really didn't, but she was nosey as fuck. After a brief stare off, she scooped the phone up, and he laughed.

"Twenty-one, twenty-five, five."

Gia punched the code in and went to the notification. Her face immediately twisted at the sight of the pretty woman playing with her hairy pussy. "Barf," she stated, and Azon peered over her shoulder.

"Damn," he marveled, and her head swiveled in his direction.

"You are nasty."

"What?" he asked with wide eyes. "I'm single, and I don't have anything to hide which is why I let you look in my phone. As you told me many times, you had a boyfriend, so I met other people. Is that wrong?"

"No, it's not wrong." Gia placed her phone down. "I'm not mad. I was just saying." She pretended to throw up.

"Don't worry. I didn't cook for her, baby," Azon smirked, and Gia giggled.

"Anyway. You might not have cooked her food, but I bet she ate that dick up." Azon didn't respond, and Gia rolled her eyes and shook her head. She still found herself smiling, however, because once again, Azon had proven to be different. She found his honesty refreshing, and it made her want to deal with him even more. She had never asked for Money's passcode, and he'd never offered. Gia was willing to bet if she did end up dealing with Azon, insecure or slighted were things she'd never feel in their relationship.

They finished in the kitchen, and Azon dried his hands and gripped Gia's waist from behind. He pulled her into him and kissed her on the back of the neck. "Do you have any more questions that need answers, or am I good to have my dessert now?" he whispered into her ear making her stomach cave in.

Gia turned her head to the side. "No more questions from me."

Azon locked his arms around her waist. "Walk."

With their bodies practically one, he guided her to his bedroom where he shut and locked the door. Gia unbuttoned her shorts and removed them along with her white lace panties. Azon licked his lips as he took in her toned thighs. His orbs traveled up to her fat mound, and his dick got hard instantly. He rolled a condom onto his dick as Gia pulled her shirt over her head and unclasped her white lace bra. Azon walked over to her with his dick sticking straight out.

"You sexy as fuck." He gently bit then sucked her bottom lip, and Gia's kitty ached for him.

She stroked his dick softly as they kissed passionately. Azon's hands massaged her ass as their tongues did a sensual dance. "Get on the bed face down ass up," he spoke into her mouth.

Gia stepped back and did as he requested. She gasped when she felt her mouth on her peach. Azon swiped his tongue down her silk folds a few times before spreading her ass cheeks and going all the way in. Gia bit her bottom lip hard enough to draw blood as Azon slurped on her pussy. He ran his tongue down the crack of her ass then locked his lips around her nub.

"My God," she gushed in a throaty moan. Gia barely recognized her own voice. Her mouth hung open, but no words or sounds came out. Her face was crumpled, and she was sure she looked crazy as hell, but she didn't care.

"Baby," she moaned as she twerked her ass on Azon's face.

"Give me that shit," he growled as he continued to lap at her pussy.

"Fuccckkk, myyyy fuckkkkk," Gia squealed as an orgasm took her breath away.

"Ummmmmmmmmm," Azon moaned into her pussy as she released her sweet nectar into his mouth.

Gia's body went limp, and she collapsed onto her stomach. Azon smirked as he spread her ass cheeks open and slid into her from behind.

"Got damn," he breathed as she moaned. Gia was wetter than he'd ever felt her, and he couldn't believe that was possible. She was so moist that he wouldn't believe he had a condom on if he wasn't the one to put it on.

Azon groaned as he pushed into Gia slowly. He began to stroke her softly, her low whimpers turning him on. "This shit too good," he moaned as he placed his chest on her back and started sucking on her neck.

He was hitting Gia's spot, and she began to tremble and whine as her pussy squeezed his manhood, and she released orgasm number two. "My God," she moaned almost as if she couldn't take anymore.

"That's right, baby." Azon kissed her ear. "Cum all on daddy's dick. This pussy juicy as fuck. You got a nigga ready to turn the fuck up in this pussy. You ready for that?"

Gia nodded feverishly as he placed her in a headlock from behind and fucked her so savagely that tears ran from her eyes. "Azon, oh my God," Gia was almost embarrassed, but he felt so good, she didn't care.

Azon turned her over and plunged back into her middle. He sucked her breasts, bit her neck, and spoke French in her ear until she was having orgasm number three. If she had any energy, Gia would have jumped up, got dressed, and took off running, because clearly, this man and his dick were the devil. But after he released into the condom, she did just the opposite. Gia fell asleep in his bed as he cleaned her off with a warm rag.

Twelve

Gia slept for three hours in Azon's bed while he went out and made money. When she woke up, she called him to tell him she was leaving, but he insisted she wait. Two hours later, he was back at home sliding into her pussy for round two. Gia almost had to fight him to get him to let her leave at three in the morning and go back to Havanna's house. She took a shower and got five hours of sleep before she got up and went to the boutique. She walked into the shop to two hundred orders, and Gia really couldn't believe that Money's infidelity was blessing her pockets the way it was. Three different trifling, messy, bloggers had found her page and tagged her. Gia refused to say anything or acknowledge the situation, but she'd gained a ton of new followers, and the orders were still coming. She had been approved for an apartment that would run her $1,400 a month, and she was moving in, in two weeks.

Gia had no clue what she wanted her second stream of income to be. She was still brainstorming on it. She was leaning towards a cosmetics line and had been looking at cute packaging. Gia knew a lot of people sold cosmetics, but people sold a lot of everything. She could sell the items in her boutique and online. She had a credit card with a five-figure limit and if need be, she'd spend a few thousand off that card to ensure that she had cute packaging and quality products. She didn't want cheap gloss that left people's lips dry. Gia also wanted lip pencils to match each shade of gloss, lashes, brow pencils, brow gel, and primer. Maybe even mascara. All the things a prissy female that loved make-up couldn't live without.

Gia was moving around like a mad woman and cursed under her breath anytime she came across an item that she didn't have. Her pieces had never sold this quickly before, and she had to stop what she was doing to order more inventory. She was busy for hours and didn't even have time to look at her phone. When she didn't have pieces in the back, she went to the front and scoured the racks for them.

"Hello," she sang when the bell above the door chimed. Gia spoke before she even looked up but when she did, she locked eyes with Azon, and she couldn't stop the smile that eased across her face as he trekked towards her with a plastic bag in his hand.

"By the time my brother came in and ate, there was barely any food left, but I managed to gather up enough to bring you."

Gia's smile widened. "How do you know I haven't eaten?"

"Because I've texted you once and called, and you aren't crazy enough to ignore a nigga, so I assumed you were busy."

"That is correct. I have orders out the ass. The only good thing about my ex being in the blogs is it drives traffic to my page and my website. Thank you so much. I've been going nonstop trying to get these orders out." Gia reached for the bag.

"Anytime. I'm about to head to the gym then I gotta go make some moves. I'll be giving Cleo too much of my time starting next week, so I have to make money now."

"I get it. Be safe. I'm moving into my place in two weeks, so I'll be able to cook for you sometimes. Especially after a hard day of training."

"I'm gonna hold you to that. When I have some time, I'm gonna slide through here and go shopping. Be easy." Azon winked at her before turning to leave.

"Damn who was that?" Jai asked making the smile instantly appear from Gia's face.

"Nobody. Nosey." She stuck her tongue out jokingly making Jai giggle. All of her employees were under the age of twenty-four. Even though Gia was only slightly older than them most of them looked up to her.

A lot of the reasons they looked up to her were shallow. She dated a boxer; she had nice things. She was pretty and had her own business. They tried to get in good with Gia with the hopes of getting into her circle and maybe meeting some of Money's friends or getting a glimpse into her personal life. That would never happen because Gia was a stickler for keeping things professional. Jai still lived at home with her parents, and she was a full-time college student. Ajonique worked part-time as a bartender and had a roommate. Khris was in esthetician school and lived with her boyfriend, and Myomi had two kids and three jobs.

Gia's boutique made decent money, but she couldn't afford to pay the girls more than $13 an hour, and none of them got forty hours of week. She knew her boutique was just a means to an end and an adult with real bills couldn't make it off her store alone. She wished she had the kind of high-end store where her employees could make commission or get at least $15 an hour but for now, the job was ideal for young adults or housewives that just wanted pocket money.

Gia completed four more orders before warming up the food that Azon brought her. The fact that he brought her food had Gia smiling too hard for her liking. Why was she so obsessed with this man when she knew it wasn't smart? Gia's taste buds rejoiced as she ate the food while looking over her website's total earnings for the day. Her cheeks lifted into a smile when her orbs zeroed in on the amount of $11,500. For the past few days, her sales had been record breaking. She almost wanted to send Money's bitch ass a thank you text message. Gia had been trying her hardest to avoid the blogs, but she did learn that Money supposedly cut Baby Cakes off for going live and letting it get out that she was on the trip with him. Hearing his name or even seeing it written made Gia's stomach turn. Just as she was finishing up her food, her phone rang, and she saw that Havanna was calling. It was crazy that they lived in the same house and barely saw each other.

"I'm off for the next three days. What's up?" she asked, making Gia giggle. She heard noise in the background.

"Where are you now?"

"In this crowded ass mall. I don't know why I even killed myself working all that overtime because this little girl just spent every last bit of it in this mall. We're on our way to the movies now, and then we're going for ice cream. Then, she's going to a birthday sleepover, and I'm in the streets. Miley, what's good?" she asked aggressively mimicking Nicki Minaj.

Gia laughed. "I'm down for whatever. What you trying to do?"

"We can hit Club Ego. They have a nice lil' vibe. Older crowd. Not too many young niggas acting an ass. I want to shake my ass not run from bullets."

"I heard that. Count me in. I'll probably be at the boutique for another two or three hours, then I'm leaving. I already have something to wear."

"Yayyyy," Havanna squealed. "I'll pick up some Don Julio on the way home, so we can pregame before. And I'll go ahead and give you a heads up. I've worked more than one hundred hours in the last two weeks. I haven't done anything but work, wash my ass, eat, and sleep. I'm getting some dick tonight, so you might want to sleep with a pillow over your ears."

Gia laughed. "Thank you for the heads up. I'll make sure I drink enough so I can come in and pass out."

The women finished up their conversation, and Gia ended the call. If the night ended the way she wanted it to, she wouldn't be able to hear Havanna have sex because she'd be in Azon's bed having some sex of her own.

***

"Yessssssss, baby!" Gia squealed dramatically as she walked into the kitchen for shots and saw the green, cowl neck dress with spaghetti straps that her friend was wearing. Havanna looked amazing in the dress, but Gia also appreciated the fact that her friend shopped at her boutique. She always made sure to post pictures and tag Gia, and because Havanna's body made the clothes look so good, Gia always got orders after Havanna posted.

Havanna was pretty popular in Diamond Cove. She'd always been popular in high school, and she was a polite person that didn't walk around with her nose in the air no matter what she accomplished. A lot of people admired that even though she was a teen mom, she was now a paid ass nurse, with a nice ass house, and when she could manage to get the time off, she stayed on flights. The great thing about Havanna was that her lifestyle was funded by herself and not a man. She worked hard to pay bills but also to live life. It was nothing for Havanna to take a girl's trip to Maimi, a week later fly her daughter to Cali, then do a solo trip to Cancun.

She was working hard to pay off her Jeep and when she did so, she was going to get a Range Rover, so she could have two cars. Havanna dated, but with her hectic work schedule and her child, she didn't have a lot of time to devote to a man and when she did give one time, and he wasted it or wasn't worthy of it, she cut his ass off quick. Being that Havanna was such an it girl, she had a lot of followers, and Gia appreciated the fact that her friend shopped with her religiously and tagged her in every picture that she posted. Having supportive friends and family was the reason that Gia's boutique hadn't failed, and she was grateful for them.

Havanna wasn't cocky, she just knew what she knew. And she knew she looked good in the dress, so when Gia started hyping her up, she did a little spin. Gia grabbed her phone. "Pour me up a shot then get ready to pose for these twenty pictures I'm going to take of you."

"You ain't said nothing but a word." Havanna was happy to see her friend in good spirits and not sulking over Money's bitch ass.

Havanna didn't do drama. She was classy, but she damn sure went in the comment section of the blogs that posted Baby Cakes video and went in on Baby Cakes. Havanna talked about everything from her veneers to her ant shape because her BBL wasn't BBL'ing. The thighs didn't match worth a damn. Baby Cakes thought she was doing something by going live with another woman's man, and Havanna was pissed.

Havanna poured the drinks, and the friends clinked their shot glasses together. "Cheeersssss!" They tossed back the shots, picked up one of the limes that Havanna had sliced and sucked on it.

"One more," Havanna spoke with her face twisted from the sour lime.

"Ayeeee," Gia swayed her hips to the beat as Latto's *Put it on the floor again,* featuring Cardi B played from the sound system. She was genuinely in a good mood, and she had her clothing sells, her friend, her sister, and Azon to thank for that. Without all that, her break-up might be harder than she was ready to deal with, but she was getting by just fine. Hell, why be sad when she had finally found a nigga that could give her orgasms?

They took the next round of shots before having a brief photoshoot then leaving the house. Three shots in, Gia was requesting an Uber because they wanted to unwind and get good and drunk without worrying about tickets or accidents. As a nurse, Havanna had seen way too many victims of drunk driving accidents. She knew better than to drive drunk and if she had more than two drinks, she didn't get behind the wheel of a car. She'd seen so many lives ruined from the people that died to the people that got so blacked out drunk, they'd get into an accident that killed five people and not even realize what they did.

Their Uber driver was an older black guy. He had a bald head and was handsome. His car smelled good, and he was driving a Tesla, so they figured Ubering must be his side hustle, and there was nothing wrong with that. He had rap music playing, and the women rapped, danced, and made videos the entire way to the club. When they got out of the Uber, Gia was in such a good mood that she gave him a $10 tip and a five-star review. The line was long so like the boss chicks that they were, they paid for the VIP line.

Inside the club, they went straight to the bar and ordered double shots of tequila. Anytime she was with Money and they came to the club, they'd always get a section, but she was no longer with Money. Sections were cool but broke or not, Gia wasn't coming up off $600 for a section. She'd stand her ass right on the floor with the regular people and still have a good time. Niggas were scamming for sections, females were sucking dick for sections, maxing out credit cards, going in with ten different people. These days, anybody could get sections really, and it was overhyped.

Gia and Havanna kept the party going as they danced with one another and hyped each other up. Gia was killing the black dress with silver sequins on the front, and her and Havanna were approached several times. Some of the guys were cute, but each of them got politely declined. Havanna just wasn't with the bullshit. She had goals to reach, and she didn't need a bunch of niggas distracting her. When she got horny, she had a man that she could call. Nyron. He lived thirty minutes outside of Diamond Cove, he was an ex-hustler turned real estate broker, and the dick was amazing. She knew he wasn't really about shit, but the dick was good, and she'd been dealing with him for two years, so she kept him around. Havanna wasn't interested in new recruits for her team just yet. Every time she let a man in, she got gravely disappointed, so she was taking a break.

Gia was fresh out of a break-up and had no desire to deal with multiple men either. While Azon had proven that a handsome man with good dick could be a great distraction, Gia wasn't about to be out here having sex like that and after a couple of dates that's what most men would want. Sex. She had already told herself if things didn't work out with Azon that she would be celibate for no less than a year. Gia believed that there was a sense of self-reflection and empowerment that came with celibacy.

The women had been partying for more than an hour when Gia had to do a double take. "Is that..." her voice trailed off as she drew back. "I have to be tripping." At that point she was five shots in, and she wasn't sloppy drunk, but she felt nice as hell.

"What?" Havanna asked and followed Gia's line of vision. "I know you fucking lying," she jerked her head back as well and eyed the pair with a face full of disdain. "Bruhhh please let me act stupid in here," she begged Gia.

Gia didn't respond because she was utterly speechless. Walking towards the rear of the club where the VIP sections were headed, was Money. But he wasn't alone. His friends trailed behind him while he had his hands on Ajonique's waist as she guided him towards the section. It dawned on Gia that this was the club that she worked at, but shorty didn't appear to be working. Their bodies were so close together that they may as well have been one. Gia didn't mix business with pleasure, but Ajonique had been working for her for almost a year. She considered her to be a cool enough person that she would hang with her outside of work if she wanted to mesh her two worlds. The very thing that she was witnessing reminded her of why she kept it cute and professional with bitches. Even though Ajonique wasn't really a friend, Gia would never ever deal with Ajonique's ex. She guessed everyone wasn't built like her.

When Gia didn't respond, Havanna knew that her friend was hurt, and she was tired of Money's bitch ass playing in Gia's face. Then he had the nerve to throw a bitch fit about Azon when he was the one out here doing the real dirt. Havanan stormed towards Money, and Gia followed. She didn't even want him to know that she cared, and if she acted an ass, he'd know just that. But she had no control over Havanna.

"You's 'bout a bitch ass nigga," she barked running up on Money so fast, that he had to stop walking abruptly. She pushed Ajonique out of the way with her hips making the girl stumble.

She looked up with a frown on her face, but when she saw Havanna and Gia, she got pale as shit.

"You better chill," Money stated in a passive tone.

"It's not enough that you're fucking bad built Instagram hoes. You fucking Gia's lil' broke ass employees. You really are a trifling ass foul nigga." She looked him up and down with a scowl on her face.

Ajonique knew enough to know that she didn't want it with Gia or Havanna, so she kept her mouth closed, but Money kissed his teeth. "She shouldn't be worried about what I do. Ain't she fucking a new nigga?" he cut his eyes at Gia while a devilish smirk covered Havanna's face.

"Hell yeah. A nigga that can make her cum with his dick and his mouth. Some shit you could never do."

"Damnn," Money's homeboy drawled from behind him while Gia's mouth fell open. Money's nostrils flared with anger.

"I don't care what that slut does."

"I bet you don't. You should really be embarrassed. A new nigga came to town. Nobody knows him and he got offered ten bands to fight you, and you running. Pussy ass nigga. You let him take your girl. You don't want him to take the title too, huh?"

"Aye you better get the fuck out my face," Money growled.

Havanna was satisfied that she had gotten under his skin. She turned to face Ajonique. "You're fired bitch."

Havanna sauntered off with Gia on her heels. "Bitch, I can't fire her for that," she hissed. "Or can I? She can't say that's discrimination or retaliation or some shit?"

"Hell no. North Carolina is an at will state. You can fire anybody, and you don't have to give them a reason. And that lil' dick sucking hoe can't spell discrimination or retaliation. She's not going to fight for that job when she's embarrassed she got caught going after your leftovers. Fuck her. I don't even want to be in this club anymore. Let's go get food."

Gia simply shook her head as she followed her friend out of the club. Her good ass mood had officially fizzled. Gia wasn't sad. More like disgusted. The more things that came to the light, she couldn't believe that she stayed with a man like Money for two years. Now, she had so many questions that she'd never know the answers to. Like did Ajonique wait until the break-up to entertain Money, or was the shit right under her nose? Gia thought about how the employees that had seen Azon had salivated over him. Anjonique's hoe ass included. It was sad as hell that Gia couldn't even let her nigga come around her thirsty ass female employees. Women were truly some savages.

Havanna looked over at Gia. "Please don't let this get you down friend. We were having a good time."

Ubers were in the vicinity of the club, so one pulled up after they'd been waiting for less than two minutes. "I'm not sad," Gia stated as they walked towards the car. "He's just embarrassing. I hate that I even dealt with him. I'm tired of seeing his face."

"That I can agree with you on."

The women headed to a wing spot that stayed open until four in the morning. Gia was still drunk, and she knew the wings and fries she was going to order were going to be good as hell. In the Uber, she checked her notifications, and she thought about the fact that Azon hadn't texted her. She hadn't spoken to him since he brought her the food. With all of the tequila that she had in her system, Gia would love to end the night riding either his dick or his face. She contemplated texting him, but the Uber arrived at their destination, and she decided to wait.

As they were walking inside, all the blood drained from Gia's face as she watched Azon walking towards the exit. He had one arm wrapped around Fallon's neck. Gia recognized her as the chick with the hairy pussy. Azon was speaking directly into her ear as they walked, and Gia wondered if he was speaking French to her.

"This just isn't my damn night," Gia mumbled. Azon wasn't her man, but she didn't want to see him boo'ed up with the next female.

"Excuse me," Fallon smiled and despite feeling as if she'd been punched in the gut, Gia smiled back and stepped to the side.

When Azon faced the front, his eyes landed on Gia, and he didn't appear to lose his cool at all. In fact, his eyes roamed her frame in the tight dress she had on. "What's up, Gia?" he asked. She wasn't sure if she was relieved or not that he didn't play her like he didn't know her.

"Hi, Azon," she smiled and kept walking.

Havanna followed her, and a small part of her wondered if Azon would abandon wolf pussy and come after her. By the time she reached the counter, no Azon.

"You okay, babe?" Havanna asked with a slightly pained look on her face. Even she was wondering why her friend kept running into things she didn't want to see.

"I'm fine, Havanna. I might not want to share dick, but I know about her. I even know her name. Azon isn't my man, and he's never lied about dealing with anyone else."

Havanna nodded glad that her friend was taking the situation so well. At least she appeared to be, but Gia's stomach was in knots. She felt foolish that she wanted to end her night with Azon, but he was with another woman. That's why she hadn't heard from him. This was the bad thing about not having a plan B. Fallon was about to go have sex, but Gia was going home alone. Life sucked.

Thirteen

The next day, Gia walked up to her parents' door with a slight hangover. Not to mention, Ajonique didn't show up for her shift, so she had to get someone else to cover it. Gia didn't really want to be at her parents' house. She wanted to be home in bed, but they were about to go out of town for four days, and her mother wanted to see her. Gia couldn't take her anger with her father out on her mother, so she decided to stop by, but she knew she wasn't going to be there long.

"Hey, babe," her mother gushed as she opened the door for Gia. "I fixed us some Greek salad, and I made salmon and rice. Let's go eat out back on the patio."

"Okay," Gia said slowly wondering if her mother was trying to keep her away from Blake. That was fine by her. Gia followed her mother to the kitchen and helped her take the food out to the screened in patio.

Gia loved being able to sit outside and enjoy the weather without bugs flying in her face and biting her. The long ass patio had a television mounted, a fireplace, a table with two chairs, and a larger chair that resembled a sofa. Gia loved her parents' house and their yard. She dreamed of having a place like that with Money one day, but shit didn't work out. She'd just have to work hard and buy her own house.

"Are you excited for your trip?" Gia asked in a cheerful tone. She truly had no issues with her mother, and she didn't want to let the fact that she was in her father's home make her awkward.

Gia's mother sipped her wine and rolled her eyes simultaneously. "No," she stated harshly and for some reason, that made Gia giggle.

"Oh Lord, what did he do now?"

Gia's mother hesitated her response. Her gaze shifted towards her plate, and she sliced a piece of salmon with her fork. That told Gia what she already should have known. It was about that person. Gia's mother placed a piece of salmon in her mouth before looking back up at her daughter.

"Work has him walking around foaming at the mouth." Mrs. Carpenter decided she'd just use the word work instead of saying Money's name because unlike her husband, she didn't wish to hurt her daughter's feelings or bring her unnecessary strife. She may have married her high school sweetheart, but that didn't mean she hadn't felt heartache. There were more than a few times when she wasn't sure they'd make it and just the thought made her breathing stifle. She could only imagine if they'd actually parted ways. She knew she would be a mess, and she wasn't afraid to admit it.

"I guess that's my fault," Gia mumbled.

"Not at all," Gia's mother responded, her tone adamant. "Don't you even sit over there and think like that. If that man doesn't have his head in the game, that's his fault. If he's out here doing reckless shit that's his fault and nobody's fault but his. I can understand Blake wanting to take this man's career to the next level, but he has to get it through his thick head that he can't care more than that person cares. He's stressing himself out over nonsense really, and it's getting on my damn nerves."

Gia could tell that her father hadn't just been getting on her nerves. "If his head isn't in the game, it's because he doesn't want it to be. I just saw Money out at the club last night, and he looked just fine to me. Maybe he should apply that same energy to the ring."

"Humph," Gia's mother huffed. "If you ask me that's part of the problem. Coming home from the club last night, he wrecked his car. The only reason he didn't get arrested and charged for driving under the influence is because the janky ass cop that arrived at the scene was a fan and didn't give him a breathalyzer, but when your father went to pick him up, the nigga was falling down, sloppy drunk. He should be his ass in somebody's holding cell right now."

"Wow." That was the only response Gia could give before shoveling some of her food into her mouth.

She didn't feel sorry for Money. Fuck him. He walked around oblivious to anyone else's feelings and how his actions affected them, so she didn't feel one bit of sympathy for him. Maybe he should man up and take accountability for his actions like Blake had suggested. Rather than trying to party and drink his pain away, he should put all of that focus and energy into his career. But Gia didn't care one way or the other. If Money failed or if he succeeded, she didn't give one flying fuck.

The topic of conversation changed to a more pleasant one, and Gia laughed and talked with her mother for an hour. Finally, she decided that she shouldn't push her luck. She'd been there long enough and hadn't had an encounter with her father. Gia knew he was home, and she wanted to go ahead and slip away before he could come outside. She didn't even have to go inside. She could have just walked from the backyard to her car, but she was going to help her mother take the dishes back into the house.

"You don't have to bother with that," her mother spoke from behind her as Gia loaded the dishwasher. "I got it. Thank you for coming to see me."

"You don't have to thank me for th—" Gia turned around, and her words stopped abruptly as *he* walked into the kitchen. He had on the same clothes as she'd seen him in the night before, but they were wrinkled, and she could tell by his sluggish demeanor and puffy face that he had just woken up.

Gia's chest heaved up and down, and her nostrils flared as they locked eyes. Money had a sheepish expression on her face, while Gia was clenching her back teeth together hard enough to make her jaw ache.

"I'm sick of seeing your fucking face. Why won't you just die already?" she barked making her mother gasp.

Gia hated the fact that she'd had such a childish outburst in her parents' home, but why did she have to keep running into this nigga? She was trying her best to get past her heartache without it getting the best of her, and every time she felt like she was doing good, the Universe kept tossing that bean head ass nigga right back in her face, and she was sick of it.

Money looked off to the side and scratched the back of his neck. Of course, he'd be humble and meek in her parents' home. Not the same cocky nigga from the club. Gia was over it. She angrily walked towards the back door when her father came in the room.

"What's the issue, Gia?"

"There is none."

Blake sighed. "He wrecked his car, and I let him come here to sleep it off. He and I have some things to discuss. I didn't even know you were coming over here today."

"It's fine. I'm leaving." Gia didn't even turn around to address her father.

With tears stinging her eyes, Gia unlocked her car and got inside. She should have listened. When her father told her that Money was off limits, she should have listened. Tears streamed down her face. Gia grabbed her phone from her purse and thought about calling Azon, but then she remembered the night before. He might be occupied still and even if he wasn't, she didn't want him hugging on her and speaking into her ear with that deep timbre the same way he'd been doing *her* just the day before.

He didn't need to be her crutch anyway. She was doing exactly what she said she wasn't going to do, and she was jumping from one man to the next. Gia swiped her tears away and turned her cell phone off. As much as she cared about her boutique, Gia was over everything and everyone. She was going to go to Havanna's house, pack a bag, and hit the highway. She didn't even have a destination in mind. Gia was just going to drive until she decided to stop. She'd then get a hotel room and figure out the rest from there. Tired of trying to be strong and numb her pain with distractions, Gia knew it was time to face the shit. She had to sit with her emotions and get through them, so she could get over them. Azon couldn't do that for her, and neither could a growing bank account. Those things were just band aids that covered her wound but didn't heal it. It was time to get real with herself.

***

Azon pulled up at the park that he was meeting Terrin at. Terrin was a mixed woman that couldn't have been older than twenty-five. To see someone his age so strung out on heroin would have been sad for Azon to witness if he wasn't already so numb to the tragedies of life. The way he saw it, everybody went through shit and the longer a person lived, the worse shit could get. There were people out there that seemed to have it all, but life didn't discriminate. That's why rich people had kids that got turned out on drugs the same way poor people did. Some people were battling cancer and other terminal illnesses while other people were suffering from being abused or raped. Life was a never ending cycle of bullshit, and if Azon walked around letting everyone's sad story get to him, he'd always feel burdened and drained.

He didn't know much of Terrin's story. He just knew that her arms were covered in track marks, so she'd obviously been using for a while. She wasn't a bad looking female, so she probably sold her body to buy heroin. On average, she hit Azon up three to four times a day, and she spent around $60 each time. There would be times she came to him with nervous looking white guys or sometimes black guys, and Azon knew that these men were buying Terrin's drugs, and she would go get high and have sex with them. None of that was Azon's business.

Terrin pulled up in an older model red car that sounded like a damn dirt bike it was making so much noise. Azon had never seen her driving before, and when he looked inside the car, he saw an older white woman sitting on the passenger side. A slight scowl covered Azon's face as she approached his car. He opened the door and got out.

"Why you always bringing somebody with you? I don't like that shit." The first time she came with one of her white tricks, Azon almost didn't serve her. For all he knew that nigga was the police, but after Azon inspected him more and peeped his dirty fingernails and the way he was all fidgety and nervous, Azon concluded that he was just a man trying to get some pussy from an addict.

"That's my mom. She cool. She wants some too. You know I'm not on that police shit." She extended a hundred-dollar bill towards him, and Azon's brows lifted.

He'd seen some wild shit, and he'd been through some things, but a mother and daughter copping heroin together was crazy to him. Azon didn't ask any questions. He just retrieved the drugs for her, and she went on her way with a smile on her face. When he got in his car and drove off, Azon wondered if he'd rather have the judgmental mother he had or one that was shooting poison into her veins. It didn't take him long to come to the realization that he'd rather have the mother that he had. He couldn't think ill of her because she didn't support his drug dealing, murderous ways. She was a good, God-fearing, hard working woman, and he still had semi-fucked up ways. Azon could only imagine how he would have turned out had she been addicted to drugs.

He'd also seen some mothers damn near push their sons into the streets because they wanted their sons that were barely even legal to be the man of the house. That was messed up to Azon too. Why keep having babies by sorry ass men then forcing your older kids to go make money to take care of the kids you made? The shit didn't make sense to him, and he didn't respect those kinds of mothers. Azon made a few more plays then, he rolled up to meet Islande, to chop it up with his brother for a few moments. With Azon dividing his time between the gym and the streets, and Islande hustling his ass off and getting pussy whenever he could, the brothers hadn't spent much time together. Fabienne was somewhere hustling like mad too.

Islande was coming out of a convenience store with a small, black, plastic bag in his hand. He spotted Azon's car and got inside. Islande had been hustling his ass off and was able to find a car salesman that would take his sister's information over the phone to get a McLaren in her name. She faxed all of the necessary documents and when she was approved, she told the salesman that her brother would be driving the car to his house until she could come down from Florida. Her information checked out, they had the same last name, and the woman paid $9,000 over the phone for the down payment. He wanted the commission on the car, and he didn't really care about particulars. The car payment wasn't cheap, but it was under $1,000 a month, and Islande made more than $1,000 a day. He was confident with getting the car, and he even had money set aside so that if anything happened to him, his sister could continue to make the payments. He didn't want to find himself in a jam and leave his sister with bad credit.

Islande got in Azon's car, and the brothers slapped palms. "You good?" Azon asked.

The one thing he hated about them selling different drugs was the fact that they couldn't hustle together and have each other's backs. They were in unknown territory, and if they were out alone, a fool might think it was okay to try them. Azon would paint the city red behind his brother, and the feeling was mutual. He had more attention on him than he wanted from that boxing shit, but the more money they made, the brothers wouldn't be able to play the background for too long. Soon, their faces would be well-known, and their names would be ringing bells. Then someone somewhere would think it was okay to come at them on some goofy shit. Azon was livid when he found out that Fabienne had been jumped and when he saw pictures of his cousin's face, he wanted to murder someone. But if anyone ever thought they'd do some shit like that to Islande and not face a gruesome death, Azon would be more than willing to show them that he was with all the shits.

"I'm good as fuck," Islande declared. "You about to go to the crib?"

"Yeah. What's up?"

"Put this money up for me that way I don't have to go back in right now." Islande began pulling wads of cash from his pockets. Azon could tell that the day had been going pretty well. There was a market for every drug. People were out here addicted to all kinds of shit but one of the favorites had to be weed. From teenagers, professionals, and even lil' old ladies, a lot of people smoked weed. One of the employees of the gas station that they were at was one of Islande's best customers. He had housewives hitting him up for dick. Shit, he had choir members hitting him up for weed the moment they got out of church. He had that good shit, and word was spreading fast. He had to go to the studio later and meet the assistant of a local rapper. Islande had never met the rapper personally, but he spent $1,200 every two or three days with Islande.

"Bet." Azon took the money and reached behind him for the Nike bookbag that he kept in his car.

"You got one more night to turn up and live life before you have to turn into a nun my nigga. You ready?" Islande smiled. He knew his brother was going to have the temperament of a rattlesnake when he had to give up weed, but he was proud of Azon. He had already called and bragged to their parents about Cleo seeking Azon out to fight a well-known boxer. They seemed happy, but Islande could tell they were skeptical. They'd have to see the fight happen in order to believe it.

Azon groaned. "I better not do all of this for nothing. Even if he can get me another fight, I want this fight. The one that's paying ten bands. If Money's lil' hoe ass will stop being scared and agree to the fight. If he was a multi-millionaire, I could see him turning his nose up at this fight, but he's not that rich to scoff at ten bands. I've seen the nigga's crib. He lives average as fuck. Why not take the ten bands for an easy win? He's so confident that he can beat me, so the fight should be short and simple."

Islande kissed his teeth. "You already know that man sees you as a threat. He can holla that beneath me shit all he wants to. A boxer only gets a certain number of fights a year. This lil' extra shit they're throwing in for him can be a lil' addition to his bank account. If it's nothing to him, blow that shit in the mall or in the strip club."

"We'll see what happens."

The brothers talked for a few more moments, then Islande got out of the car but not before they agreed that they'd hang out later. It was about to get real for Azon, and he was going to have to be disciplined and focused. Before he drove off, he decided to text Gia. She was the last person that he expected to run into the night before when he was with Fallon. He was actually out, and Fallon texted him because she saw him, and she made her way over. Azon caught a flashback of how good that pussy was, and it was a no brainer that he was going to go back to her place and get some of that. He hated that Gia had to see it, but he hadn't done anything wrong. Azon stood by the fact that he was single. He protected himself, and he wasn't out here lying to anyone. He couldn't quite read the look on Gia's face. She didn't look mad, but with women you could never tell.

It crossed his mind to get rid of Fallon and hit Gia up, but he didn't want to do that either. That would mean that he was getting too close to Gia. She was fresh out of a break-up and though he was a fuck nigga, Azon knew that Money was still in her heart. You can't just stop loving a person. Azon wanted to give her time to fully get over Money. If they did end up falling into something, he didn't want baggage from her situation with him spilling into what they were trying to build. Azon wasn't against relationships, but he didn't make it his mission to be in them either. He knew how he was. Most men wouldn't admit it, but he knew if he ever found the woman that could inch her way into his heart, he would love her hard. Hard as fuck. Because of that fact, Azon had to be very selective. He couldn't fall for a woman with extreme issues and baggage. He couldn't fall for a woman like Khloe that would sex his man as soon as his back was turned. He couldn't fall for a liar that was juggling multiple men and would put him in the position to have to kill or be killed.

Falling for the wrong partner could ruin a person's life, and Azon didn't have time for that. For that reason alone, he was going to keep his options open and take things slow with Gia. If he had to choose, he'd say she was his favorite, however. By the time Azon reached his destination fifteen minutes later, Gia still hadn't responded. Maybe she was busy. Maybe she was in her feelings. Only time would tell.

Fourteen

Gia checked her watch as she glided her feet back and forth in the water. Gia was sitting by the pool soaking up some sun and enjoying the quietness of the morning. She had spent two nights in Atlanta, and the getaway was much needed. She checked into a five-star hotel and got in the hot tub in her room right away. She went out for breakfast, lunch, and dinner each day, and she would read books on her Kindle app while she ate versus scrolling social media like she normally did. In the hotel room, she would sit in silence, read, or look at inspirational YouTube videos. Her phone was on do not disturb, so no calls or text messages came through. Phone calls could only came through if the same person called back-to-back, and so far, no one had done that. Gia refused to even check her emails. When she said she wanted a break from everyone and everything she meant it. Her body was still loose from the massage she had gotten the day before in the hotel's spa, and she knew she'd put on a few pounds from all the eating she'd been doing. It was super hard for her not to have a drink or two, but Gia had sworn off alcohol for a few days. She only wanted to do what was good for her and not just what felt good to her.

Luck was on her side because she was able to squeeze in a last minute appointment with one of the city's most popular lash techs. Gia got her lashes and nails done while she was in the A, and she topped it off with a pedicure. Her credit card got swiped one too many times at Lennox mall, but Gia didn't care. Yes, she was about to move into a new place, but she deserved to treat herself too. She'd worry about later, later. It's not like she was broke. Being on her own for the first time was a little intimidating, but Gia knew she was just overthinking. Even if her boutique stopped making money tomorrow, which it wouldn't, she would just go find a job. She'd bite the bullet and ask Blake for a loan. She'd do anything but be homeless and carless. Gia was too much of a hustler to let that happen.

Gia sighed as she pulled her feet from the water. It was time to head back home and get back to reality. The chance encounters with Money, the random sightings of Azon and his women friends. Finding out people weren't who she thought they were and being blamed for things that weren't her fault. It was time to head back to all that, but at least now, she had a clear head. The silence had done her some good. Writing in her journal, praying, and reflecting had done wonders for her soul. Despite all the bad, she still had a lot to be thankful for, and that was what she would focus on. When she got back home, she'd start interviewing people to take over Ajonique's position, and she'd start buying décor for her new place. She also needed to hit the gym and work off all the calories she'd consumed in the A.

Which reminded her that finding a new gym was on her list of things to do. Gia wasn't mad at Azon for being with Fallon. He hadn't done anything wrong. The fact that she cared made her realize that she wasn't sticking to the script that she was supposed to, and she didn't like that. She just needed to step back for a bit and regroup. If she could go a few weeks without seeing his face, hearing his voice, or riding that dick, she could prove to herself that she didn't have an unhealthy attachment to him.

She also knew that he was about to be very busy training with Cleo. Even if Money didn't agree to the fight, Gia hoped that Cleo could get Azon some paid fights, so he could hopefully spend less time in the streets and more time in the ring. Gia prayed that he would get to the level where he could make really good money and leave the street life alone for good. Whether they ended up being in each other's lives or not, there wasn't one bad thing she could say about Azon, and she truly wanted the best for him.

Gia packed her bags wishing she could stay a few more days, but she had to get back to life. The orders hadn't slowed down much for the boutique and for that, she was grateful. Since midnight, she'd already had seventy orders. Before Money and his side chick made it to the blogs, a very good day for her was around forty online orders. An average day for her was around fifteen online orders. The tea had started to simmer down, so Gia hoped that the new people that had discovered her really liked her merchandise and would be repeat customers.

In the car, Gia blew out a deep breath and took her phone off DND. The messages and missed calls popped up, and she saw that her mother, Havanna, Azon, and a few other people had called and texted her. Gia texted everyone back except Azon and let them know she had just needed a few days to herself, but she was on the way back home. She didn't text Azon because Gia needed some more time away from him. Her lil' vacation that included a slight detox from bad habits included a detox from Azon, and she needed to extend it for a lil' bit. He needed to focus on boxing and if he needed something to occupy his time after that, she was sure Fallon was available.

As soon as Gia arrived back in Diamond Cove, she stopped by her boutique, and she was pleased to see that there were three customers in line at the register and five people browsing around the store. Gia had made up her mind to go ahead and get her cosmetics line popping. She was going to get someone to make a logo and when she got back to Havanna's she'd order the products and work on a website. She wanted the cosmetics website separate from her boutique, but she would have the website listed on the boutique's site since it was her more popular website. Gia would also make a display in her boutique where people could come in the store and purchase the items.

Gia spoke to the employees and the customers and checked the bank bag. There was $7,000 that needed to be deposited in the bank, and Gia silently cursed herself out for leaving that much money in the boutique unattended. She was going to go through every transaction and make sure all of the money was accounted for. Gia hated to think she might have had girls working for her that she couldn't trust but clearly, some of her employees didn't feel like they owed her any kind of loyalty or decency. Gia busied herself with catching up on work, and she didn't look up from the computer for the next hour and a half and then it was only because someone knocked on the door.

"Come in."

Khris walked into the office with a sheepish expression on her face. "Hi, Gia."

"Hey. What's up?" Gia's tone was pleasant, and there was a smile on her face.

Khris and Ajonique were what she'd consider to be friends. Whenever they worked together, they were always talking and giggling, and Gia knew they hung out sometimes after work. Gia wasn't even the type of person that went around fighting, but if she ever caught wind of Ajonique dealing with Money while Gia was with him, she just might dog walk that hoe. If something had only started between them once Money was single, no matter how trife Gia thought it was, she'd leave well enough alone. And whether Khris and Ajonique were friends or not, Gia refused to be mean or angry. That's not the kind of boss she was, and she would treat all of her employees with respect.

"Yesterday, I asked Ajonique why she didn't work here anymore, and she told me that you saw her with Money. I just want you to know that I had no idea. I swear I didn't know anything about them." Khris's eyes were wide, and the girl almost looked afraid.

Gia shook her head, "Khris, I'm not worried about that. I can assure you. I never bring my personal life to work, and I don't let what happens outside of work affect my boutique. I didn't even technically fire Ajonique, my homegirl said that. If she would have shown up to work, I probably would have let her. Money is single, and he can do what he wants. I expected more from Ajonique, but we aren't friends, and she doesn't owe me anything."

Khris shook her head. "I know you're professional, and you treat us nice, but you make it clear that we aren't friends. And I can get why. Because a lot of people try to become buddy buddy with the boss, so they can get over. You're never mean to us or rude even when you catch us doing stuff we shouldn't be doing. I feel like she did owe you something. She was wrong, and I'll tell her that to her face. I just wanted you to know that I didn't know."

Gia smiled. "It's okay, Khris. Thank you all for keeping things running smoothly while I went out of town. I really appreciate having dependable employees. If things stay like they are with the online orders, I may do some evaluations and give raises. I know I can't pay much, but I do what I can."

Khris's facial muscles relaxed, and she stopped looking so nervous. "Thank you, Gia. We appreciate you too."

Khris left the office, and Gia got back to work. One conclusion that she came to on her vacation was that she was going to stop letting Money, Ajonique, her father, and anyone else disturb her peace. She was taking a page from Azon's book. She wasn't compromising her peace for anybody. They could all get the hell on.

***

Azon was serving Terrin when Nice approached his car. Azon had seen the man a few times since he'd robbed him, and he looked worse each time. Nice losing an abundance of money didn't stop his drug use at all. It simply fueled his hustle, and he got the funds for his heroin anyway he could. If only he knew that the heroin he'd been buying from Azon was purchased with the money that Azon and Fabienne stole from him, he'd be hotter than fish grease.

"Azon say man, let me get $60 worth. I got this nice ass gold chain. She something nice to look at," Nice pulled a gold rope necklace from his pocket and laid it across his ashy, calloused, palm for Azon to see.

Azon glared at the necklace then shifted his gaze towards Nice's face. His body was sore as fuck from working out with Cleo, and he hadn't had any weed in damn near twenty-four hours. It would have made Azon's day to get out of the car and beat Nice's ass. But he wasn't going to do that. After a few moments of silence, he stared directly into Nice's eyes and parted his lips.

"Get that shit the fuck out my face."

Nice kissed his teeth in frustration before standing up straight and pulling wrinkled bills from his pocket. Knowing that he had the money, but he'd wasted time showing Azon that bullshit necklace, had Azon even more pissed. "You just begging for me to beat yo' ass," Azon glared at the man. "I should refuse to serve yo' ass since you like to play games."

It had taken Nice way too long to earn $60, and he was seconds away from getting dope sick. He danced in place in an effort to keep his guts from bubbling. When Nice got dope sick, the first symptom that hit him was diarrhea. His body didn't care where he was or who he was around. His bowels would release everywhere, and he didn't want that to happen on the block.

"Come on man. Don't do me like that. You know I had to try."

Azon served the man just to get him out of his face. He was exhausted and since he'd made more than $1,500 since leaving the gym, he was tempted to take it in, but it was early, and he wanted to at least see if he could make $2,000. This was the main reason that Azon didn't want to put all of his energy into training. Taking his body through all the bullshit for $10,000 when he could make that from hustling was borderline insane.

Azon looked down at the watch on his wrist and saw that it was only five PM.

"Hell nah, you not going to sleep yet," he mumbled to himself even though he'd been up since five that morning. He still had a few more hours in him before he went home to shower and go to sleep.

It crossed Azon's mind that it had been five days since Gia saw him with Fallon. He'd texted her three times since then and called her once. With everything he had going on, Azon damn near didn't have it in his heart to sweat her ass, but he decided to see if she was at work, so he could find out what her problem was. When he spoke to her that night of course, Fallon started with the interrogation. She wanted to know who Gia was and how Azon knew her, and he ignored every question she tossed his way because he didn't have to explain anything to anyone.

When Azon pulled up at the boutique, he saw Gia's Kia parked out front. He grunted as he pushed his sore body from his car and winced as he stepped inside. This shit was for the birds. Azon was in pretty good shape, or so he thought before Cleo got ahold of his ass. He could barely move. Azon knew he wasn't supposed to be taking any kind of drug or alcohol, but he was tempted as fuck to see if he could find a Perc. He then decided against it because he knew there were a lot of fake pills floating around the streets, and he wanted no parts of it.

Azon stepped through the door of the boutique, and one of the employees greeted him with a smile. "Welcome to Pretty Fly." The young woman was smiling hard at him and one thing that stood out to Azon was that everyone employed in Gia's boutique was attractive. None of them made his dick brick up like Gia though.

He nodded at the person that greeted him while his eyes darted around the room in search of Gia. He spotted her near the back of the store smiling in some nigga's face. His back was to Azon, but he could see Gia's gorgeous face perfectly fine.

"Are you looking for something in particular?" The salesgirl approached him, and his eyes left Gia's face and fell on the woman in front of him.

"Nah. I came to see your boss." Azon's gaze shifted back in Gia's direction, and she was staring at him with a surprised look on her face.

Not one to cause a scene, Azon simply smirked and headed for the back of the store where the men's clothing was located. He walked past Gia and the guy that she was talking to and began looking through clothes. He'd only been looking for a few moments, and quite a few pieces had caught his eye. Azon liked finding nice fly pieces that didn't look cheap and were something besides Polo, Dior, Fendi, Gucci, and Balenciaga. He would wear all those brands, but he wanted something that everybody else wasn't rocking.

He picked up one of the shirts that he liked and glimpsed at the price tag. Forty dollars wasn't bad at all. He smelled her intoxicating scent before she opened her mouth. "Hi," Gia spoke, and Azon turned to face her with eyes so dark, she almost took a step back. He'd never eyed her with so much fury. Her mouth fell open, but no words left her mouth.

"I did something to you?" he gritted serious as ever. This was a side of Azon that she'd only seen the night that he was barking on Money. His wrath had never been directed at her.

"No," she admitted in a soft tone suddenly feeling silly for ignoring him.

"Yeah, I can't tell. I've texted you and called you quite a few times. An I'm busy, kiss my ass, or anything would have sufficed. Got me hitting you up like a goofy ass nigga, and you're ignoring me, but just bounced your fake ass over here talking about hi all cheery and shit."

Gia's brows hiked. He was really telling her off, and she wasn't sure if her feelings were hurt, or if she was turned on.

"Fake? Azo—"

"Nah, I'm good on all that," he cut her off with a kiss of his teeth. "I just needed to lay eyes on you and make sure you were okay but since I see you're fine, and you just like to play games, I don't have shit to say. I'm not that Money nigga," he growled before turning his back on her and going back to shopping.

Gia's breath hitched in her throat. He had read her for filth, and she didn't know what to say. When she spoke, her tone was low because she didn't want anyone to hear her begging.

"Azon, I'm sorry. The day after I saw you and Fallon, I went to my parents' house and Money was there. Before I saw you that night, I saw him with one of my employees in the club, and I was already in a bad mood. I saw you and got a little jealous, and when I saw him the next day, I just exploded. I knew then that for my own sanity, I just needed to get away. I went out of town for a few days and left my phone on do not disturb. I'm sorry," she repeated meekly.

She stood there feeling helpless while Azon ignored her for a few more minutes. After he'd grabbed a few more items, he turned back to face her. "If you were jealous, respectfully, that's your problem not mine. I'm not going to apologize because I wasn't wrong. You said you weren't looking for anything serious, so if you can't handle dating, maybe you need to stop. And as far as Money, fuck that nigga," Azon spat in an aggressive tone. "One thing I won't ever do is be on the receiving end of your bad moods because of something that fuck nigga did. I have no problem treating you with respect, honoring your feelings, and communicating with you like an adult. I'm never ever being punished for the last nigga though. When you get your mind right, Gia you know my number."

Azon walked towards the register leaving her stuck on stupid. Gia was truly stunned. She was used to Money flipping out on her out of guilt. He used to try and make her grievances with him seem unwarranted and stupid, but Azon actually had a reason to flip. She felt childish as hell, and if he never wanted to speak to her again, it would be her own dumb ass fault.

The moment Azon told Gia off, he felt better. "I need some muhfuckin' weed," he chuckled to himself.

After he paid for his things and left the boutique, he felt a little bad. She did look sorry, and she was sexy as fuck giving him those sad eyes. She'd been dressed in grey sweats, with a grey fitted tank top that showed off her belly. He loved when she wore baggy bottoms and tight tops. It made her look like a sexy ass tomboy. Azon wanted to take her in her office and bend her ass over.

He would have rather punished her with dick than words, but he was too tired for that. Plus, Gia needed to learn not to play with him. He fucked with her for rea, but she really had to let all the shit with Money go before he could invest himself. The point of what they were doing was to learn each other, and she had learned this fuckin' day that Azon wasn't the one.

The night before at the gas station, a sexy ass redbone had approached him and asked for his number. He was giving Gia's heart time to heal. That didn't mean he wasn't going to have fun in the process. It would be up to her how much fun he had.

Fifteen

Havanna's mouth hung open as Gia recanted to her the things Azon said to her the day before in her boutique. "Close your damn mouth before a fly flies in," Gia rolled her eyes at Havanna.

"Damnnnnn. Him getting all savage on you and shit didn't make your pussy wet?"

"As hell," Gia confessed, and the women erupted into a fit of giggles.

"Girl," Havanna fanned herself as if she was hot. "I'd be over there having all kinds of make-up sex. You better put your pride to the side and call that man."

Gia pouted as she picked up one of her wings. "Ughhhhh," she groaned dramatically. "I'm not used to being the fuck up. I said sorry twice. I'm not in the habit of begging niggas," she frowned.

"Well, friend you were wrong. You know I don't be cutting these men no slack but so far, I like Azon for you. I'm not telling you to rush into anything I'm just saying, you aren't the only female in Diamond Cove that can tell that man is different. Don't let these thirsty, hairy pussy hoes, trick you out your spot."

Gia giggled. "I'm not telling you shit else."

Havanna frowned. "If it's about hairy pussy please don't."

"Oh myyyy gahhhhh," Gia groaned in a deep voice as three men walked through the door. "Diamond Cove is not that damn small. God hates me!" she hissed harshly as Azon looked her way.

Havanna smirked. "It's either Azon or hoe ass Money, and it better not be hoe ass Money."

Gia didn't reply, but Havanna got her answer when Azon came over to their table, leaned down, and spoke into Gia's ear. "You still mad at daddy?"

She hated the way her clit throbbed. Absolutely hated it. "No," she mumbled.

Azon moved his face over to hers and pecked her on the lips. "You sure?" he peered into her eyes, and all she could do was nod, and he pecked her two more times. Gia damn near had an orgasm right there.

"Well damn," Havanna marveled from across the table of the popular wing spot they were in. The women loved the restaurant because it served the best frozen alcoholic drinks. Even the virgin slushies were fire on a hot day. Their drinks were similar to the popular bar Wet Willie's.

Azon looked over at her and chuckled. "My name is Azon. You must be Havanna."

"I must be," she declared still impressed by the way Azon came over and shut shit down.

With a smirk on his face, he eyed the wings, fries, and the large frozen drink in front of Havanna. "However much your food and drinks are, I got it. I need somebody on my side when this one gets to acting crazy and shit," he glanced back at Gia who bashfully looked down at her food.

"I was just in here telling her how she was dead wrong, so I'm already on top of that, but you can damn sure pay for my food."

"It's nice to know you'll be quick to throw me under the bus for some food."

"And will," Havanna drew back. "Don't act like you don't know."

"I like you already," Azon jerked his head to the left. "This is my homie, Fabienne, and this is my brother Islande."

"Hello," Havanna smiled lowkey eyeing Fabienne. He was fine and had a body to die for. If he was anything like Azon she wouldn't mind riding that ride.

The men spoke, then he introduced them to Gia. He then lowered his voice, so only him, Gia, and Havanna could hear. "I'm going to order my food. By the time I'm done, I know you'll be done, and then we're leaving to go to my crib."

Gia's brows furrowed. "Are you asking me or telling me?"

"I'm telling you," he responded coolly before walking off.

Havanna pumped her fist dramatically. "I like that nigga." She hissed a little too hype for Gia's liking.

"Okay calm down, Miss," Gia chuckled.

"Hell no I won't. In fact, if you keep messing up with that man, I'll disown you my damn self. You know I can spot a fuck nigga for everybody but myself. I wasn't trying to be a Debbie Downer when I told you three months in, I didn't think Money was the one for you. I wasn't being a hater. I meant that shit but Azon. Baby you better fall in love with that man and have his kids."

Gia shook her head. The same effect Azon was having on Havanna was what Gia had felt. She wasn't sure if she was being naïve or delusional when she kept pegging him to be different. If Havanna could see it, Gia was comforted by the fact that she couldn't be tripping. Azon was good people, and she made a promise to herself not to mess things up by doing the most. By the time Azon sat beside her with his food and drink, Gia and Havanna were done eating, and Havanna was ordering her and Gia another drink.

Islande and Fabienne sat at the table beside the booth that Gia, Havanna, and Azon were in. "You full?" Azon glanced down at the six bones on Gia's plate. He knew she was a woman, but he didn't see how six wings and some fries could fill anyone up. Especially when they were drinking.

"Yeah. I had a burger a few hours before we came because I knew I'd be drinking."

"You might as well order some food to go 'cus you know you gon' be hungry later. You 'bout to drink some more, and I'm gon' work yo' ass out for sure," he ogled her body lustfully while she blushed.

Gia had missed him so much so, that she leaned in and kissed him on the lips. Gia heard commotion in the background, and she looked over and saw Money and a few of his friends. People were stopping him to ask for pictures, but he was mean mugging Gia and Azon.

"The universe fucking hates me," she declared, and Azon turned to see what she was looking at.

Azon chuckled and bit into a wing. "That nigga mugging me or you?" He looked from Money to Gia. "'Cus if he knew what was good for him, he'd find something safe to do." Even though Money was across the room, Azon spoke loud enough for Money and everyone else in the restaurant to hear.

One of Money's minions, stepped forward like he was about to do something, and Islande stood up. "I been bored all day. If you want to get some shit crackin' let's go," he stated with an evil grin that made Money stretch his arm out and keep his friend from going closer.

"These muhfuckas aren't worth it," Money spat.

"Is that why you're scared to fight him?" Havanna sniggered, and Money took a step towards her.

"I'm 'bout sick of your slick ass mouth, bitch."

It was Fabienne's turn to stand up. "You need somebody to teach you the manners that yo' mammy didn't in this bitch?" he gritted.

Azon sat back in the booth with a smile on his face. "Be easy homies. The only way I'm beating this nigga's ass is for ten bands. I mean, he won't agree to the fight, so he must know he can't beat me, but I refuse to fuck him up for free."

Money looked Azon up and down. "Nigga, you're a fucking nobody. They want me to fight you on some undercard shit. Do you know who I am? You're beneath me."

"If I'm that irrelevant, you should be itching to get an easy ten bands. Nigga you drive a G wagon and live in a town house. You not doing it that big," Azon stated with a look of disgust making a few patrons of the restaurant laugh which pissed Money off even more.

"This will be the first and the last time I ever resort to fighting a dusty ass nobody in the ring. I'm gon' beat yo' ass so bad muhfuckas won't be able to recognize you," Money glowered, and Islande laughed.

"Nigga you funny as fuck. I got five bands that says my brother will straighten your crooked ass nose. What's good?" he held his dick and stared at Money.

"Nigga, fuck you," Money kissed his teeth.

"Okay save it for the ring," the owner called out nervously not wanting the rambunctious crowd to mess up his establishment with a brawl. "Whoever wins though, you can eat here free for six months," he promised, and Azon nodded.

"I'll be looking forward to that."

"Let's go," Money told his friends, and Gia breathed a sigh of relief.

Azon looked over at her with a chuckle. "Fuck you nervous for?"

***

An hour and a half later, Gia was glaring at the back of Azon's head with a frown on her face. "Azon! I know you're really not about to go to sleep without giving me some dick," she pouted. When he didn't respond, she smacked her lips together. "I'm going home."

Azon turned to face her. "Your spoiled ass ain't going nowhere. Damn, you can't sleep beside me without having sex? That's all you want me for?"

She rolled her eyes because she was tipsy and horny, and he was playing. "No, but it's been a minute, and I'm horny," she whined.

Azon laughed. "You a big ass baby. Your ass is on punishment for how you acted. I haven't forgotten." He frowned slightly, and Gia remembered that she had been a lil' fucked up.

"I'm sorry," she moaned in a sexy voice. "Let me make it up to you."

Gia got on her knees and grazed her hand across Azon's crotch. His member was soft and still thick and heavy. Her mouth watered as she reached inside his boxer briefs and pulled his dick out. She took him into her mouth hungrily, and Azon's teeth sank into his bottom lip. The drinks she'd consumed had Gia on go, and it didn't take long for Azon to grow in her mouth. He moaned and wrapped his hand around her braids as she gagged from deep throating him.

"Do that shit," Azon groaned.

Gia sucked him like a woman with a point to prove. She really was apologizing with her mouth, and it had his toes curling. Azon's lids were damn near closed as his chest heaved up and down from the pleasure.

"Suck that dick," he groaned making her moan and hum on his pipe.

Gia pulled a bold move as she cleaned all her saliva off of Azon and straddled him. She didn't wait for him to get a condom as she placed his fat mushroom tip at her opening. Azon looked up at her. "Yo, you do this shit, and I can't promise you I'm gon' be able to pull out."

As if she didn't care Gia eased down on his dick making them moan simultaneously. Just as he assumed it would be, her pussy was some fire with no barrier between them. She was so tight and wet that Azon feared he would cum embarrassingly fast. He couldn't smoke or drink, and Gia's tight, slippery folds had him feeling like a virgin all over again.

"Fuckkkk," he groaned as she moved her body back and forth and rode him slowly.

"I missed you so much," she moaned before leaning down to snake her tongue into his mouth. The alcohol in her system made Gia let go of all of her inhibitions.

"Word?" Azon licked his lips and gripped her waist. "I missed you too." He spoke against her lips.

Gia's eyes fluttered closed. She was in heaven. Being with Azon felt like being on top of the world. She'd been very smitten with Money in the beginning of their relationship, and there were times that she was very happy. But the way Azon made her feel was so foreign to Gia that it was insane. What was this man doing to her?

Azon took control and flipped her onto her back. She caressed the back of his head and moaned as he drilled into her middle. Gia wound her hips underneath him and met him thrust for thrust. Hearing Azon curse and groan was like music to her ears and when her stomach spasmed, and her legs quivered from an orgasm, that was all it took. Azon released into her with a growl knowing the only way he would have been able to pull out was if someone put a gun to his head.

"Not smoking weed or drinking got me nutting fast as hell," he mumbled with his eyes closed.

Gia could feel his heart racing as they lay chest to chest. She pushed out a light chuckle. "That wasn't what I'd call fast. You lasted at least fifteen minutes. That's good enough for me. The guy that took my virginity came after three strokes. That's what you call fast."

Azon climbed off of Gia's body. "I still wanted to lay up in that pussy for at least twenty-five minutes, but it's all good."

Gia noticed him wincing. Though she was exhausted, she wanted to ease his discomfort. "After I clean up, why don't I give you a massage? You look like you're constipated."

Azon laughed. "I'd rather be constipated than barely able to move. But you can do that."

They took turns cleaning up in his bathroom and moments later, Azon was flat on his stomach while Gia straddled him and sat on his back. She applied the right amount of pressure to soothe Azon's aching muscles. What she was doing to him felt so good, he found himself moaning every few seconds.

"Fuck, I need you every night," he groaned.

"I could make that happen." Gia wasn't sure if he really meant it, but she'd come whenever he called, and that was a fact. Yeah, she'd done it. She had managed to fall, but she still knew that they needed to take their time. Rushing in the past had gotten her feelings hurt. She was so fixated by the good that she chose to purposely ignore the bad instead of confronting it and dealing with it. The thought of that person not being in her life made her accept certain things until she couldn't accept them anymore. Had she dealt with them in the beginning, it would have saved her a lot of heartache. Lesson learned.

Five minutes into the massage Gia heard light snoring, and she snickered. She knew Azon was tired, and she was so happy for him. It was almost sad how much he didn't recognize his own talent. Fast money was always appealing but in her heart of hearts, Gia knew that Azon could go far if he remained patient and stayed focused. If fighting Money was the way he had to get his foot in the door, then so be it.

Sixteen

Azon walked out of the gym with a scowl on his face. His body was less sore than it had been days before, but he was still drained, and all he wanted was to go home, take a hot shower, and smoke a blunt. He wasn't going to do it though because Cleo had been tossing compliments his way during their entire session, and he stated more than once how much Azon's timing and stamina had improved. He was able to see that the man was no longer smoking weed or drinking alcohol. The boxing drills he'd done earlier had almost frustrated him because Azon was just used to getting in the ring and doing whatever to get the pressure off. He didn't care too much about perfecting his techniques, improving his footwork, or anything else associated with boxing on a professional level.

Cleo had him doing things he'd never done before and when Azon didn't catch on right away, he got frustrated. But he would never back down from shit, so he'd focus until he got it right, and Cleo's eyes would light up like the sky on the Fourth of July. He was so invested in Azon that he was ready to invest some of his own money and take this man around the world with him until somebody gave him a real chance. He could start out doing undercard fights before main events and work his way up from there. Whatever he had to do Cleo was with it. He just needed to make sure that Azon remained focused. Cleo hated to judge, but he could tell from the man's aura, attitude, swag, hair, and gold teeth that he was into some illegal shit, but Cleo couldn't ask Azon to blindly walk away from what was paying his bills. Before he could fix his mouth to do that, he would need to bring Azon some solid promises and not just hopes and dreams. The $10,000 was a good start, but it wasn't the end all be all especially not when the car that Azon drove made Cleo aware that making $10,000 on his own probably wasn't too hard for the young man.

"Excuse me young man."

Azon almost kept walking, but something told him that the voice he heard was directed towards him. He lifted his head squinting from the son and saw a caramel-colored older gentleman coming his way. It wasn't hard for Azon to peep the man's swag and he knew that in his prime, this nigga was probably somebody. As his freckled face came closer, Azon squinted his eyes. This nigga looked like somebody he knew.

The man extended his hand towards Azon for a shake. "Hello. My name is Blake Carpenter, and I'm assuming you're Azon."

Azon bit back a sneer as he extended his hand. He had no desire to shake the man's hand, but with the way he was sexing and nutting all up in Blake's daughter's womb, they just might be family one day.

"What's up?" Azon grumbled. He wasn't sure what Blake wanted with him, but he wasn't up for the bullshit. He might come at Gia sideways, but Azon was a grown ass man. He doubted this was a friendly visit because Blake was on Money's dick so bad he may as well have been fucking him. There's no way he saw Azon as anything other than an enemy.

"I understand that in the heat of the moment, Money agreed to a fight that I told him not to. A man can't go back on his word, but I can assure you that

Money isn't thinking clearly. He's thinking off emotions rather than logic. This might be a game to you, but boxing is Money's life. I'm trying my best to keep him from sinking, but he's not making my job easy. From what I gather, this would be your first fight, and you don't even take boxing serious. I'm going to do something I've never done before. If you'll agree to throw the fight with Money, I'll pay you $15,000. That's five thousand more than you would get for the fight."

Azon stared at Blake for a moment to make sure the man was serious and when he saw that Blake was, he laughed in his face. "I got up at five this morning, and I've been in this gym for the past three hours busting my ass, and I don't take this serious? Respectfully, you don't know me. You don't know a thing about me because if you did, you'd know I'm not a hoe. I can't be bought. Fuck I look like throwing a fight and making myself look stupid for fifteen bands?" Azon's upper lip curled. The man was disgusted at this point; he had no respect for Gia's father.

Blake's face turned red, and his jaw muscles flexed. "I used to be young, cocky, and arrogant, and it didn't get me far. You and Money can engage in this pissing contest all you want. I'm out of the shit. I'd just appreciate you staying away from my daughter."

Again, Azon laughed. "I'm trying really hard to remain respectful because I like your daughter, but I'm a grown ass man and last time I checked, Gia was a grown ass woman. You can't tell me shit." Azon looked Blake up and down before walking off.

He knew how some females were with wanting their man and their families to get along. Gia wasn't his girl, but he already knew that should they ever take it there, there would be tension with her father. Azon didn't kiss ass, and he didn't need Blake's approval. If Gia could get that through her head they might be able to progress but so far, in Azon's eyes, Blake was a sucka ass nigga, and he had no desire to know the man.

***

Azon entered his house and when he did so, Fabienne and Islande stopped talking abruptly. Azon peered at the men. Fabienne gave him a head nod while Islande pulled from the blunt he was holding. "Why y'all stop talking like some hoes? Y'all throwing me a surprise party you don't want me to know about?" Azon's temper was still on a hundred. Not being able to smoke weed was blowing him something terrible.

Islande chuckled as he blew weed smoke from his lungs. "Because what we're talking about doesn't concern you."

Azon glared at his brother. He wasn't an emotional person. He left that for females. His brother was grown and didn't have to tell him shit, but that's not how they got down. Azon knew if they were being secretive, it was because they felt it was some shit he wouldn't approve of. Hating how much he sounded like his mother, Azon looked over at Fabienne.

"You already know I'm not letting you drag that lil' nigga into no shit," he stated in a firm tone. He loved Fabienne like a brother, but he'd go to war with that nigga behind his *real* brother.

Fabienne shook his head. He would have told anyone else to suck his dick, but he already knew how Azon was about Islande, so he didn't take the comment personal. "How you know it's not him dragging me into some shit?" he asked calmly with his head cocked to the side.

Azon dropped his gym bag on the floor and sat down on the couch. "Islande, I'm really not with the shit," he gave his brother a warning.

"You and this grumpy shit ain't talking 'bout nothing. I'm about ready to hop in the ring with yo' ass." Islande kissed his teeth. "Nigga asked me if I knew anybody trying to buy some ki's of coke. I told him nah. I know coke is Fabienne's thing, but I'm not hollering his name to just anybody. Dude goes on to tell me this his cousin from Philly is on the run. If the nigga is on the run for real, he has an idiotic ass cousin telling too much of his business. But it seems the nigga was babysitting his girlfriend's nine-month-old daughter while she went to work. I won't go into specifics, but she came home, and the nigga was gone, and her daughter wasn't breathing. Shorty had skull fractures and all. You figure out the rest," Islande's jaw muscles flexed. The shit made him so mad, he refused to tell the whole story.

Azon's nostrils flared, and he bounced left leg anxiously. "Where this bitch ass nigga?" He wanted to know. He was pissed off and ready to take some of his frustration out on a nigga.

"He got in town about an hour ago. I told Noonie that I'd ask around, but I'm for damn sure going to act like I couldn't find anybody. This nigga wants off the bricks so bad, he's selling them for $10,000 each, so he can go on the run somewhere. I don't know how many he has, but I'm gon' take them shits. After I kill his ass," Islande gritted. "Nigga is keeping a low profile. I think he has a room at an Extended Stay hotel on the south side.

We didn't tell you because you need to be focused on this fight. We got this."

"Nah," Azon replied adamantly. "Three heads are better than two. Fuck that fight. You know how I give it up. This nigga, he deserves this shit. I want in. I want in bad as hell."

"Bet. I'm about to take Noonie some weed. I'm gon' try to get more info on where this nigga is. If I do, I'll let y'all know, and we can take it from there. It's gon' be harder to get the bricks if he has them in a hotel room, but we'll figure something out."

Azon and Fabienne nodded as Islande stood up to head out. That was one reason that Azon didn't want kids by a woman he wasn't with. There could be too many different kinds of men around his child, and he'd do a hundred years in prison for killing a nigga that violated his. It wasn't about the bricks or the money in this case. He wanted to kill the nigga because he deserved it. The bricks and the money were an added bonus. While they waited, Azon told Fabienne about Gia's father, and Fabienne laughed.

"They really think you're a thirsty ass nobody. He wanted you to throw a fight for fifteen bands? That nigga smoking dick."

"They gon' learn quick that assuming some shit about me isn't going to get them anywhere. I'd really hate to have to knock his old ass out because Gia would probably never speak to me again, but he better steer clear. I'm not about to play with his ass."

"Fuck that old ass nigga. Speaking of Gia, you know what her friend Havanna on?"

Azon shrugged passively. "Not really. Gia is about to move into her new place. She's staying with Havanna for now, and I've been by there once. It's a nice ass crib. Shorty is a nurse and has a kid. That's all I know."

Fabienne stroked his chin as he nodded. "If I run into her again, I may have to see what's up with that."

"Not if you gon' be on bullshit because you know how women stick together, and I don't want to hear Gia's mouth."

Fabienne laughed. "Bullshit? Nah. But you already know I'm not looking for a relationship though. I don't trust a bitch as far as I can throw her, but I'll trick a li' bit and give her some good ass dick."

"On that note, I'm going to take a shower." Azon stood up making Fabienne laugh.

Fabienne was serious, however. Khloe and Janay had left a bad taste in his mouth. He wasn't a sucka for love ass nigga that fell in love after a few conversations, but Janay had a mean ass talk game. They'd only been dealing with each other for two months before she bought him an expensive outfit, some cologne, and some sneakers for his birthday. She was always cooking for him, and her pussy was good too. Janay catered to him, and he actually felt guilty on the nights that she wanted to see him, but he was with Khloe. Both women acted so in love with him and wanted so much of his time that he didn't have room for anyone else on his roster. Between his welding job and selling weed, time wasn't something that Fabienne had a lot to give.

Juggling the two of them had become a lot, and he was trying to decide which one he would keep and who he would let go. Before he could make his decision,

Taj and Chris jumped him, and he hadn't spoken to Janay since. She had assured him more than once that her and Taj were done. She claimed that she hadn't had sex with him in more than six months, and that he had a new girlfriend. Fabienne didn't know if that was true or not but what he did know was, she should have never had him in her house if that nigga had a key.

Khloe was initially upset that Fabienne had been with another woman when he was attacked. With the pain that he was in, he couldn't care less who was mad, and he wasn't in the position to coddle Khloe or kiss her ass. After about two weeks, she came around and assisted his mother and sister in taking care of him. They got closer with her being by his side, and she won the role of his girl by default. Khloe was heartbroken when Fabienne beat Taj almost to death and went to prison. She had been by his side through his injury and his bid, so although a relationship wasn't what he wanted to come home to, he couldn't do her dirty. Until he found out that like Janay, she wasn't shit either, and just like that Fabienne was done. Relationships weren't for him, and he was okay with that.

There were plenty of women out there that didn't mind flings, sneaky links, friends with benefits, whatever title they chose. Fabienne had no issue with providing women with pleasure and then dipping out and not hearing from them until they needed another release. If he could find a woman that was fine with it, he'd be in heaven. He wasn't a broke nigga, so he didn't mind paying for hair, lashes, hell, he might even pay rent or a car note, but he wasn't spending time outside of a nut, and he didn't do love. As long as that was understood, things would go smoothly. If Havanna could fuck with that cool. If not, he'd just admire her sexy ass and keep it moving.

Azon had perfect timing because as soon as he entered the living room from his shower, Fabienne was ending his call with Islande. "The nigga found someone to buy the bricks," Fabienne reported to Islande as he stood up. "He's with his cousin, Noonie, and Islande heard him say he had to go to the hotel room to get the bricks. We're going to head to the hotel. Islande is going to figure out what to do because if Noonie stays with the nigga, he can't come. Unless we kill Noonie too."

Azon nodded his understanding. His Glock stayed on him at all times, so all he needed before leaving out of the door was his ski mask. Noonie wasn't Islande's friend, but they were cordial. The men could be savages, but they weren't completely heartless. Azon knew that his brother wouldn't want to kill Noonie if he didn't have to. Fabienne drove to the hotel hoping things would go smoothly. Not only did he want to avoid prison, but he really wanted to see Azon make it in boxing. He prayed his cousin didn't become one of those ones that got the slightest taste of success before it was snatched away. This street shit was risky. It could bring a person instant gratification, or one simple action could ruin a person's life forever. Each lick was a gamble with life and freedom.

Islande called Azon and let him know what kind of car Reggie was driving and what he looked like. He also stated that Noonie didn't tag along because he had an appointment at the barber shop, so Islande was on his way to the hotel too. Traffic was kind of thick, and Fabienne silently prayed that they wouldn't miss him. Islande wasn't sure of where Reggie was going to meet the guy that wanted to purchase the drugs. When

Fabienne arrived at the Extended Stay, he saw a man that fit Reggie's description going into a side door, and a smile eased across his face.

"Got him." He rubbed his hands together while Azon pulled his weapon and screwed the silencer on.

"Any idea where we gon' take this nigga?" he asked Fabienne. He didn't want to just rob the man, he wanted to kill him too, and they couldn't do that at the hotel.

"I'm thinking on it."

Two minutes passed, and the man hadn't come out of the building yet. Islande arrived, parked his car and hopped out. Since he had already met Reggie, he was going to approach the man and say that he knew some guys that were willing to pay way more for the bricks than what he was asking. Islande posted up and waited for Reggie to emerge from the building. A minute later, he did. Fabienne and Azon watched as Islande approached the man, and he instantly stepped back. He was on the run and had a lot of drugs in his possession. It was natural for him to be on guard and untrusting. The men saw Islande hold his hands up in surrender as if he was trying to convince Reggie that he posed no threat. He jerked his head towards Fabienne's car and let Reggie know that he'd told the men that the bricks were going for $15,000, and they wanted five if he had that many.

Islande had the gift of gab and though Reggie was skeptical, he ultimately let greed lead him towards the car, and that would be the biggest mistake he'd ever made.

"What up?" Reggie asked Fabienne nervously as he walked up to the driver's side window.

Fabienne didn't want to come off as threatening, so he made sure to keep his tone polite. "What's good, homie? I know you not trying to do business out in the open like this. You can get in the car. We done bite."

"I was thinking we can do the business up in my room." Reggie wasn't stupid. He wasn't willingly getting into a car with three men that he didn't know.

Islande stood directly behind Reggie as Azon brandished his weapon. "What you gon' do," Azon spoke up. "Is get yo' ass in this car. There's a gun behind you and two in front of you. You have way more to lose than we do. Being that you're on the run for murder and all. We can get yo' ass or the police can get you. Your choice."

Reggie didn't want to die, but he knew the kind of torture he would endure in prison for harming a child. He felt stuck. A part of him wanted to run and call the men's bluff. Would they really shoot him in the back in broad daylight? When he was about to take off, Islande delivered a blow to the man's kidney that made him double over and drop the bag of drugs on the ground. Islande picked the bag up and yanked the door open simultaneously.

"Get in the fucking car," he growled, and Reggie did as he asked.

"Man, just please let me go," Reggie groveled as Fabienne pulled off. "I don't have any money. The drugs are all I have. If you take the drugs, I'll be assed out. I'm fucked up. I may as well go ahead and turn myself in. Just let me live."

"Did you let that lil' girl live nigga?" Islande barked.

"That was an accident. She wouldn't stop cr—"

Islande hit the man in the face so hard, everyone in the car heard the bone in his nose crack. "You about to sit up here and try to explain that shit to me?!" Islande roared and hit the man again. He was livid, and Reggie was gon' feel all of his anger.

"Don't get blood in my car," Fabienne stated calmly as he glanced over his shoulder. "Got damn, Islande," he kissed his teeth when he saw the man's nose was leaking like a faucet.

"It's on his clothes not on the seats." Islande turned towards Reggie. "If any blood gets on my man's seats, I'm not gon' kill you. I'm gon' torture the fuck out of you and leave you lying somewhere until you die, and that could take days."

Reggie continued to snivel while Islande, Azon, and Fabienne ignored him. He had done the unthinkable, and no one felt sorry for what was about to come to him. None of the men would ever be cold hearted enough to kill a child. No matter the circumstances. Not purposely, and they wouldn't even be able to live with themselves if they did it accidentally. That was the main reason none of them ever shot blindly. Bullets didn't have names, and shooting into houses or crowds was a no no.

Fabienne drove for almost thirty minutes before he pulled up in the middle of nowhere. Reggie had been afraid for the entire car ride but being driven into a desolate area with nothing but tall grass and dirt roads had him ready to lose control of his bladder.

"Pleaseeeee," he screamed at the top of his lungs as Islande dragged him out of the car.

They were out in no man's land, but that didn't mean that no humans could be in the area. Islande didn't appreciate Reggie screaming, and a blow to the back of the head made the man's knees buckle and sent him crumbling to the ground. Azon walked around the car and kicked the man in the mouth sending blood, teeth, and saliva flying. "Get yo' big bad ass up," he glared down at the man that was on the ground curled up in a fetal position.

"This pussy not gon' get up," Fabienne predicted before stomping the man in the stomach and causing him to urinate all over himself.

"Oh you not gon' get up?" Azon kicked him in the face again.

All Reggie could do was throw his hands up and try to block the blows while crying like a baby, but nobody felt sorry for him. Just days before, he'd taken his frustration with life out on an innocent soul, and karma was coming back to him tenfold. As he lay on the ground, Reggie silently repented for his sins and prayed that death would come quick while the men continued to kick and stomp him. After a minute, they had grown bored, and they had better shit to do than to keep playing with Reggie. Azon pointed his gun at the man's face and let off four silent rounds. Islande wanted so badly to spit on the man, but he didn't want his DNA on the man's body.

Back in the car, Fabienne drove like he had some sense because they had guns and drugs on them. "See how many bricks that nigga had," he instructed Islande.

Islande opened the bag and counted the square packages that were stacked inside. "Nine bricks."

Fabienne gave a slight head nod. "Bet. I'll get one of my customers to test it and if it's some good shit, I know whole bricks could go for no less than $20,000. Of course, we can make more money if we bust those bitches down. I know neither one of you sell coke, so I can get off the work for you and just give each of you $60,000. Cool?"

"Works for me," Azon nodded while Islande agreed too.

They couldn't be mad at $60,000 for murdering a baby killer. They would have done that for nothing. Azon sat back in deep thought. With the $60,000 that he had, the money he had stashed, and the drugs that he had left, he had a nice sum of money. Nice enough that he just might be able to sit back and focus more on boxing and less on hustling. But the money that he had wouldn't fund his gym *and* pay his bills. Fight money was mediocre for an amateur like him, but Azon was smart enough to know that he couldn't keep playing around in the streets and think nothing bad would ever happen. He might have to make a choice.

By the time he made it back to his car, Azon had customers waiting on him, and Gia had called him twice. He called the money back first and went and made each sale before showing up at her new apartment. Gia answered the door dressed in black shorts, and a cropped black matching shirt. The braids had been removed, and her natural hair was piled on top of her head in a messy bun. When her eyes landed on his face, she rolled her eyes at him, and he shook his head as he stepped over the threshold.

"I was busy, Gia," he explained while closing the door behind him.

"Ummhmmm," she went back to the kitchen and continued putting her dishes away. "It's cool. I got a guy that lives on the first floor to bring the boxes up."

Azon's brows furrowed. "A guy that stays on the first floor?" he eyed the short shorts she wore that barely covered her ass cheeks. "Don't get fucked up, Gia. Whether he lives in this building or not, you don't need to have strange men up in your crib especially when you're half naked."

Gia kissed her teeth in response. "If you're jealous that's your problem," she repeated his words to her, and Azon pushed out an angry chuckle.

"I'm not jealous at all, baby. I can't be jealous over what's not mine. I'm simply telling you that what you did isn't smart."

Gia's face burned with embarrassment from him stating he wasn't jealous. "I've done a lot of shit in my life that isn't smart. You're just one more that's added to the list."

Azon was trying his best to keep his cool. Islande had pointed out many times that him not being able to smoke weed had him acting worse than a woman that was suffering from PMS. "I was fucking busy," he growled in a low tone. "I get that you're a princess, and you like to come first in a man's life, but I have bills to pay, and I have shit to do. My world doesn't and won't ever revolve around one person. You need to let that brat shit go."

Gia shook her head. "And that right there was lesson number one on why you never open up to a man. I didn't expect to come before Money's boxing career, so let's not go there. I was his biggest supporter. I didn't want him in my face all day every day. I simply wanted him to act like I mattered! You don't get to throw what I told you back up in my face. Secondly, I know what time you left the gym. Excuse the fuck out of me for wanting you to be careful and safe and smart. Because I know what your being busy consists of, but as of today, I don't give a fuck. Play in the streets, sell drugs, do whatever it is you want to do. I only care about me. You can get the fuck out of my crib now."

Azon didn't do the arguing shit. He wasn't beat for it. Gia wasn't even his girl, so standing in her apartment engaging in a screaming match was some shit that he didn't have time for. He had better shit to be doing like making money, so she didn't have to tell him twice. Azon turned his back and left.

Seventeen

"Ughhhhhh," Havanna groaned and kicked her legs like a child having a tantrum. "He won."

Gia sipped from her glass of wine and giggled. "I told you to stop looking at posts about that fight."

Money had won the infamous fight that her father told her he'd lose if he didn't get his head in the game. It seemed that he must have gotten himself together because though she didn't care to keep up with the fight, Havanna was, and it seemed that Money had won. Now, in a few weeks, he was set to fight Azon. Gia was surprisingly pretty much over Money, but Azon was another story. They hadn't spoken in a week, and though it made her sad, Gia felt that might be best. She was doing too much too fast. She needed to be focused on her boutique and her cosmetics line, and he needed to be focused on boxing. Gia had launched the grand opening of her line, and she got nine hundred orders in three days. Havanna had come over to help her pack the orders, and they were due for a wine break once they were done.

"I can't help it. I wanted him to lose so bad," Havanna groaned, and Gia laughed.

"I hate Money almost as much as you, but don't wish bad on him, friend. We don't want that energy to come back on you. We don't care if he does good or if he does bad. Fuck him."

"What the hell ever," Havanna rolled her eyes. "Anyway. I know you haven't, but I'm going to ask anyway. Have you spoke to Azon?"

"Havanna," Gia stated her tone thick with warning.

Havanna held her hands up in surrender. "Friend, I'm giving you grace. I love the energy you're putting into your boutique and your cosmetics line. I see you bossing up on another level, and I love that for you. Trust me when I tell you that a man is not the end all be all, but I don't think you two should end on a bad note. Just still at least be friends."

"For the moment, Azon and I need this time apart. I don't hate him, and I hope he doesn't hate me, but I need some time. Can you please stop saying his name and making it a big deal? Whatever is supposed to happen will."

"I'll back off," Havanna gave Gia a small smile.

"Thank you."

The women finished off the bottle of wine, and Havanna left to go home. After Gia climbed into bed, she lay on her side staring at the wall, her mind thinking a million different thoughts. It hurt her feelings when Azon called her a brat and insinuated that she was wrong in how she felt. She was simply worried about him. He wasn't the type to break promises and when he didn't show up or text her back, she felt something could be wrong. She wanted the best for Azon because she was a decent person, but she had clearly overstepped her boundaries. She wasn't used to dealing with a dope boy, and her fear regarding his safety came out in the form of an attitude. When it came to that, her and Azon kept bumping heads. If his impression of her was that she was a spoiled, childish, brat, she hated that she gave him that impression, but what could she do?

Gia's last relationship hadn't been a healthy one. All she knew about most relationships was that they were hard work. No one was perfect, and it took her a long time to give up on Money. Her and Azon weren't in a relationship, so maybe he didn't owe her anything, but in Gia's world, you didn't give up on people that you cared about. Their wires kept getting crossed, so for the moment, she was going to refrain from reaching out to him. Maybe she needed to work on her communication skills and learn how to get her point across without coming across as a brat. After she'd done the necessary work on herself, then maybe she'd reach out. Only time would tell.

Gia just knew that she couldn't keep going in circles. Something had to give. And while she didn't view her break-up with Money as her fault, that didn't mean that she didn't have flaws that she needed to work on. Gia wanted her mind to calm down and stop racing because she had to go to dinner at her parents' house the next day, and if she was tired or had a headache, it would make the experience that much more exhausting. Gia thought it would be a long time before she stepped foot back on her parents' property, but it was her father that wanted her to come over, and her mother had begged her to come hear him out.

Gia couldn't imagine what he wanted to say to her, but since Money won this fight maybe he was in a good mood. Good mood or not, the first time he came at her wrong, she was going to set some boundaries in the most respectful way possible Gia closed her eyes and waited for sleep to come. Who knew what tomorrow would bring?

***

Gia inhaled a deep breath before walking out into her parents' backyard. Her mother, Kaylin, and her maternal grandmother were all in the living room. After talking to them for about twenty minutes, Gia decided to bite the bullet and go see what kind of mood her father was in. It was tempting to avoid him for as long as she could and just mingle with her other family, but the anxiety was killing her. Gia slid the glass patio door back and walked down three steps. Blake looked over his shoulder and actually smiled at her.

"Hey, Gia. How are you doing?"

"I'm fine, daddy." She went and stood beside him as he flipped steaks, chicken, and hot dogs. "You're in a good mood."

Blake chuckled. "It seems that way, huh? You know I approached that Azon character at the gym and offered him $15,000 to throw the fight with Money."

Gia's eyes widened at her father's revelation. "You did what?"

Blake pushed out a hearty laugh. "You heard me. I thought I was gon' have to knock that lil' nigga out. He looked me square in the face and told me he wasn't a hoe." Blake laughed again, and Gia was truly stunned. You would think Azon cursing him out was the funniest thing in the world.

"Okayyy," she replied slowly still confused.

"As much as I've put into advancing Money's career, I have to respect a real man, and Azon is that. I can't ever deny his talent because even rough around the edges with no real formal training, the nigga is a problem in the ring. I can't be mad at that. All I can do is respect that. For him to be virtually unknown and for this to be an undercard fight and his first fight, the fact that he didn't fold for the money impressed me more. When I confronted Money about sneaking around with you, he couldn't even look me in the eyes. He was stuttering and giving me bullshit excuses. Azon isn't backing down from me, Money, or anyone else, and that young man is alright with me. Whether you two remain friends or start dating, I'm good either way. And after a lot of nights of your mother refusing to talk to me, I can see that I've been nothing short of an asshole, and I'm sorry."

Gia's brows lifted from shock. Her father just kept right on blowing her mind. She had no idea he'd offered Azon money to throw the fight and the fact that he was suddenly cool with her dating Azon was shocking too. It didn't much matter because they weren't even speaking, but what did matter to her was his apology. Blake was stubborn as hell, so she was just going to take the apology and let the past be the past.

"Thank you, daddy. I appreciate that. I see Money won his fight last night."

"Barely," Blake grumbled. "I'm trying to be patient, but it's taking everything I have in me not to tell that man to go jump off a bridge. Now, he's throwing a fit because I found a kid out in South Carolina to work with. Money doesn't bring me in enough revenue for him to be my only client. The only reason that I could even survive with him being my only client this long is because I have my own money but fuck that. I may be retired from boxing, but I still hopefully have at least another thirty-five years on this earth. I need to be bringing more money in than I have going out. If he can't handle me working with other clients, he's free to leave. I'm sick of his temper tantrums."

All of this was new to Gia, but she wasn't surprised at all. She really didn't even care to keep talking about Money. She honestly didn't care what he had going on in his life. She stood outside with her father for another ten minutes until the food was ready and finally for the first time in months, Gia had a relaxing stress-free dinner with her parents, and it felt good. When they were done eating, she even laid around in the living room, and they all watched a movie. A text message came through her phone from a number that she didn't recognize, and Gia's brows snapped together as she read the long message.

You're right, I was a bad boyfriend. I see that now. I was so focused on my career and going to the next level that's all I really cared about. You were begging me to change, and I was confident that you'd be there. In my mind, I'd get to where I wanted to be in boxing, and then I would work on us. I was stupid, and I took you for granted. That London shit was lame as fuck, and I'm ashamed. My homie had been wanting to get at this chick bad as hell, and he knew she'd be in London with her friends around my birthday. He wanted to fly out there on some stuntin shit, and I let him get me caught up. I was not fucking with that girl prior to that trip. Please just come back home. I swear to God, I'll change. My life hasn't been the same since you left.

Gia frowned as she deleted the message and blocked the number that Money had texted her from. It was too little too damn late. Maybe he really wanted her back. Maybe he wanted to mess with Azon's head before their fight. She wasn't sure what was going on, but she didn't want any parts of it. The chapter with Money had come to an end. When the movie was over, Gia told everyone good-bye, grabbed her to go plate, and walked out to her car with a smile on her face. Life wasn't perfect. It never would be but for right now, she was at peace. She had completed her goal of having two streams of income, and they were both doing well. Her father had apologized to her and for however long it may last, they were on good terms. Her waist got a lil' smaller while her ass got a lil' fatter. She loved her new apartment. Gia refused to complain about anything.

Even though it would have been nice to go home to some dick, Gia refused to dwell on that. Remembering her promise to herself made her groan. She had said if things didn't work out with Azon she would be celibate for a year. Gia shook her head from the reality of not having sex for a year. Maybe it would do her some good, but got damn she wasn't looking forward to it.

Eighteen

Azon gritted his back teeth together as Fallon's eyes lit up when she saw that they were across from Gia's boutique. They had met for lunch, and she mentioned that her birthday was coming up, and she wanted some shades and other items for her upcoming trip. Azon offered to buy them for her because even though he'd been focused on his upcoming fight and sex hadn't been at the forefront of his mind, Fallon still drained his balls whenever he needed her to, and she did a damn good job of it. Azon hadn't seen or spoken to Gia in three weeks, but he thought about her often. Going up in her place of business with another woman didn't sit right with him. He wasn't trying to rub anything in her face or make her feel bad. Azon parted his lips to tell her he'd wait outside when Gia walked towards the door.

She smiled at him and Fallon and opened the door. "Are you guys coming in?"

Fallon recognized her immediately and wondered if she was the reason why he'd been hesitant to go inside. Fallon wasn't generally a petty person, but she was on Azon. Real bad. She wanted him to be hers, and she felt vindicated once again running into this woman that he knew while he was by her side.

"Yes we are," Fallon replied in a chipper voice. "Come on, babe. They have the best accessories."

Gia continued to smile as she held the door open for them. "Thank you," Azon gave a slight head nod as he walked past her.

He followed Fallon around the store for a bit, but he couldn't keep his eyes off Gia. She had walked behind the register and was talking to one of her employees. On her tomboy shit again, Azon's dick bricked up at the sight of her in baggy, black Cargo shorts, a white muscle shirt, and black strappy heels. She had ginger-colored faux locs in her head, and shorty was badder than a three-year-old.

"Bae? You like these?" Fallon asked trying to get his attention.

Azon kissed his teeth annoyed. "What's with this babe and bae shit. You never called me that a day in your life," he finally stopped looking at Gia and focused on her.

Fallon was slightly taken aback at the way his dark eyes pierced through her. "Damn. I'm sorry. I'm just happy you're taking me shopping. Is it a problem?"

Azon reached inside his pocket and pulled out some money. He counted out $200 and passed it to Fallon. "I'll be right back."

Her jaw slacked as she watched him walk towards the woman with the faux locs. Fallon wasn't mad at getting $200, but Azon had her fucked up. Azon approached the counter halting Gia and Khris's conversation.

"You don't miss me?" he asked her boldly.

The gentleness in his tone and the sincerity in his eyes melted Gia's heart, but she refused to show it. Her eyes narrowed as she glared at him. "Sir, I haven't seen you in three weeks, and you're in here with another woman. Please don't play games with me."

"Answer the question."

The way he was staring at her was damn near making Khris moist. The spectacle was an interesting one, but she walked away to give Gia some privacy. Shit, boss lady stayed winning because this man was way better looking than Money. And according to Ajonique, Money had had sex with her once and refused to pay for her Uber home. Khris couldn't help but laugh and told her that's what she got.

Gia stared at Azon trying to figure out what kind of games he was playing. She never again wanted to feel like she loved a man more than he loved her. It had to be equal or nothing. She wasn't up for men that got a kick out of having their egos stroked by how much a woman let them get away with. This wasn't that.

"'Cus I missed you. I missed the fuck out of you."

"I can tell," she stated in a small voice, but the sarcasm still peaked through.

"That ain't 'bout shit. I promise you that."

Azon rounded the counter and tongued Gia down so aggressively that, "Got damn," was heard from Khris.

Azon gently bit Gia's bottom lip and placed his lips on her ear. "Je ne veux personne d'autre que toi."

"I don't know what that means," she whispered as she tried to steady her breathing. Her panties were uncomfortably moist, and she wasn't acting professional at all, but Gia didn't care at the moment. She could feel Fallon's eyes on them.

"It means I don't want anybody but you." His mouth was still against her ear, and the bass in his voice made her tremble.

She pulled back, so he would look into her eyes, and she searched his face for clues that he was telling the truth. "If that's the case, handle that." She didn't have to elaborate because he knew what she meant.

Azon walked back over to Fallon who looked mad enough to spit nails. "You can keep the money, but that's my girlfriend now. I'm sorry, but I can't fuck with you anymore."

Fallon's eyes narrowed into slits, and she clenched her fists at her side. "Fuck you, fuck her, and fuck this cheap ass store," she hissed before storming out.

"Damn why my store gotta be cheap?" Gia chuckled.

Azon walked back over to Gia and pressed his body directly into hers, and she could feel his hard member through his jeans. "Take me in the office now, or somebody is going to get a show."

He didn't have to tell Gia twice. Moments later, her panties and shorts were on the floor while her heels remained on. She was bent over the desk in her office, and Azon was behind her with her pussy in his mouth. Gia's eyes were closed, and she whimpered in ecstasy as Azon sucked and licked on her plump, freshly waxed mound. His tongue felt so good sliding down her center. When he stuck his finger in her ass, Gia's knees buckled, and she came instantly. Azon feasted on her essence as her body trembled, and she clawed at her desk. He got as much of her honey as he could, but there were still remnants of her orgasm running down her thighs.

She was still chest down on the desk breathing hard as hell when Azon slid into her from behind. "Oh my gahhhhh," she cried out in a deep, raspy voice. She had missed his ass indeed. No way could she have been celibate for a year with dick like this walking around.

Azon smacked her ass roughly. "No more not talking for days shit. No more poor communication. We fix shit before we go to bed, aight?" he asked and smacked her ass again so hard that he left a handprint.

"Yes, baby," Gia moaned as her body continued to convulse.

"This my pussy?" he asked as he grabbed a handful of her locs.

"Yes, baby. Oh my God, yes," Gia threw the pussy back at him, and Azon yanked her head back roughly as far as it would go, so he could get his tongue down her throat.

They engaged in a nasty, sloppy, tongue kiss that had her cumming again, and that orgasm sucked the seed from Azon's dick. "Got damn," he marveled. "I can't wait until I can drink again. I'm on yo' ass."

He pulled his shiny tool out of Gia, and she rushed to the bathroom to clean up the mess that he'd made. Even after all of her essence had been cleaned away, her yoni was still contracting. She wanted more of Mr. Laplanche. After he washed his dick off, he came back in the office and said what she was thinking.

"I'll be over there tonight around one. I have to do something first."

"Yes sir."

***

Azon walked into the Internet Café with $28,000 in his possession. That was his share of the money that was taken when he and his crew robbed the place. Even though they were a different nationality, the couple reminded him so much of his parents that out of all the crimes he'd ever committed this one bothered him the most. Azon just couldn't shake the feeling, and he knew what he had to do. He couldn't walk up to them and admit to robbing the place, so he would take the $28,000 and gamble with it. Azon sat there for almost two hours mindlessly feeding the machine. He got frustrated when he won $1,800 because he didn't want to take anything. Luck was on his side though because after sitting there for hours stuffing the machines, he'd won $3,500. Azon decided he would take that. As long as he'd given the original $28,000 back, he could rest easy.

Maybe he was finally growing up. He felt good when he walked out of the Internet Café. His fight with Money was coming up, and Azon couldn't believe that it had been almost two months since he smoked a blunt or had a drink. He knew this fight would determine how things went moving forward. Because of that, he was hesitant to give up his heroin clientele, but Azon was hustling just enough to bring in at least $1,500 a day.

Azon stopped by the grocery store on his way to Gia's apartment to get her a bouquet of roses. He smiled at the thought of her. It had been two days since they made up, and he'd busted no less than four nuts. She was draining him, but he but he wasn't complaining. He had a key because sometimes he came in late, so when he let himself in, she was in the kitchen sipping wine, listening to music, and cooking. When Azon walked in the kitchen and saw the bright orange spandex shorts that were hugging her ass cheeks, he drew back.

"Got damn that ass sitting."

Gia giggled and turned around. Her eyes widened when she saw the flowers. "Babe! I got two separate deliveries today."

"I know. Before I could order you some when you moved in, we got into it. So, you needed a dozen for the living room, the kitchen, and the bedroom."

Walking over to him with a huge grin on her face, Gia wrapped her arms around his neck. She placed a juicy kiss on his lips before taking the flowers from him. "You are so sweet. Thank you. Are you ready for tomorrow?"

"As ready as I'll ever be."

Azon was slightly nervous but not that Money would beat him. Shit, he was twenty plus fights in, realistically he should beat Azon. It had been stressed many times that Azon was a 'nobody' so why should he be embarrassed if he lost the fight? Azon was just wondering if he'd be able to step back from dealing and actually pursue this boxing thing. He wanted to say it didn't matter. If he had to continue selling heroin that's what he would do, but was it what he wanted to do? He was floored when Islande made him aware that their parents and sister were coming into town to watch the fight. That was a big ass deal for Azon. He was shocked that his parents' approval meant as much as it did to him at his big age, but he finally wanted to give them something to be proud of.

Gia fixed his plate and handed it to him. "Okay you have to go to bed early tonight. You have to be well rested for tomorrow, and we can't have sex tonight."

She was so serious that it made Azon laugh. "Yes sir, boss."

"I just want everything to go smoothly tomorrow. You know what's so crazy is that everybody is talking about this fight? This is going to be the event of the year. People are more hype for this fight than they've ever been for any of Money's fights."

"Oh yeah?"

"I promise you. The venue sold out last week, and people are mad as hell that weren't able to get tickets. I swear, nobody in their right mind would be able to tell that Money isn't fighting someone on his level careerwise."

Azon didn't need any more pressure, so he took her words with a grain of salt. "Damn that's what's up."

They ate their food, Azon showered, and went to sleep, and it wasn't even ten PM, but he had a long day ahead. He didn't know how in the hell the next night would end, but he knew he'd be good either way. It was just that for once, he had made a goal. He finally wanted to stop playing with boxing and take it serious. He just couldn't be sure that it would go how he wanted it to.

Nineteen

Gia chewed on her bottom lip nervously, and her heart pounded in her chest. It was nearing the end of round one, and Money and Azon were going toe to toe. She could tell that Money was focused, but he was also getting tired. She knew him well and could read his body language. Everyone was shocked at how well Azon was hanging with Money. Blow for blow, they were both fighting like they were in their prime. Money hit Azon with a body shot that made her breathing stall, but Azon came back with a fury of punches that made the crowd go wild as the bell rung. Round one was over.

"Azon can box, bitch," Havanna marveled. She was to the left of Gia, and Islande was to the right of her. Then there was Fabienne, Johanne, Jeane, Azon's parents, and Angeline.

"I know. Even if he doesn't win, I know he has people's attention, and he should be able to get another fight easy."

Gia's breath hitched in her throat, and her nerves were on ten again as the second round started. She quickly observed that Money was running, and she concluded that he was trying to tire Azon out. As soon as she thought it, one of the commentators called Money out on it. Gia glanced at her father, and Blake's red face told her that he was pissed. Meanwhile, Cleo was on the opposite side of the ring, coaching Azon from the sidelines.

Money finally stopped running and hit Azon with a two piece that made Gia cringe. He could definitely hold his own, but she was beginning to wonder if he would actually win. He was damn good, but Money was an experienced boxer and Azon was not. The second round ended, and the fight was intense if nothing else.

"My nigga got this," Gia heard Islande say as round three started.

Round three went much like the previous round and by the fourth round, Gia could tell that Azon was tired too. The fight was very close, and it looked like either man could win but near the end of round four, Azon caught a second wind that damn near gave him super-human strength. Gia along with others in the crowd gasped as blow after blow reigned down on Money. When Money fell backwards onto the mat, the majority of the crowd jumped to their feet as the countdown began. Gia thought her heart would leap out of her chest as the referee hit number one, and Azon was declared the winner by knockout.

The crowd was going insane. She wasn't even thinking about her dislike for Money. All Gia could think about was what this win would mean for Azon, and she was elated. Many thought he couldn't do it, but he had. When they got Money off the floor and eased on the bench, he came to, and Gai knew he would be embarrassed. Embarrassed and pissed. When the event was over, Gia waited around outside with everyone that came to see Azon fight.

"That was good," Havanna gushed. "Money didn't even last five rounds. Blake 'bout to rip that man a new asshole."

"That sounded real gay," Gia laughed.

"Yeah it did."

When Azon finally came out of the venue, his parents and his sister rushed over to him. Gia watched with a smile as they conversed, and his father even hugged him. She let everyone get their time in because she would sure get hers later on that night. She already had a blunt rolled for him and some tequila chilling in the freezer. It was going to be a long, fun, nasty night.

When he was finally done talking to his family, Azon walked towards Gia with a crooked grin on his face. "What's up?" he asked, and she jumped into his arms.

"I'm so proud of you," she kissed him on the lips.

"Cleo told me he can get me lined up for another fight in eight weeks. That one is paying $7,000," he grinned. Yeah, it was lower than what he got for fighting Money, but Azon was on his way. Gia knew it, and he did too.

"Looks like we gotta work on getting that gym open," Gia gazed into his eyes. "I'm so freaking proud of you."

"Thank you, baby."

Truth was, Azon was proud of his damn self. He never saw boxing in his future when he came to North Carolina. He may still sell heroin until his next fight, but Azon had already made up his mind, that the selling drugs would be coming to an end soon. Of course, he knew Fabienne and Islande would still be doing their thing, and that was their business. Azon would never judge, but he simply felt it was time for him to take a different route.

Azon stood around talking for a while and then finally, he was ready to go. He walked towards his car with Gia by his side. In the car, he looked over at her and asked his customary question.

"You good?"

Gia leaned over and kissed him on the lips. "I'm better than good, baby."

The end! Flip the page for my catalog and who do you think will get a story next, Islande or Fabienne?

Natisha's catalog:

Billionaire Status

Uri's Interlude: The Cezar Cartel Vol. 1

Ballad of a Gangsta's Girl: The Cezar Cartel Vol. 2.

Isa's Verse: The Cezar Cartel Vol. 3

The Outro: The Cezar Cartel Vol. 4

Tales of a Menace

Savage

Tales of a Gangsta

Noelle and Star: A Shotta's Wife

Let it Burn

From the Trenches with Love

Tarai & Jahan: Stronger than Pride

How the Baptiste Boys Took Over North Carolina

The Baptiste Boys Ultimate Box Set Experience

A Gangsta and His Shawty

The Return of the Baptiste Boys

Kisses from a Savage

Finessing the Opps 1-2

In Love with the Hood in Him

Cuffed by a Southern King

Islam and Azzure: Lovin' the Plug

Azaan & Jayda: Fallin' for a Haitian Hitta

Addicted to a Heartless Hitta

Cuffed by a Southern King

Kisses from a Savage

Diary of a Mafia Princess 1-3

Married to a Haitian Mob Boss

Southern Thugs Do it Better

Shawty Got a Thang for Them Country Boys

The Allure of a Thug

For the Love of You

Money

Power

Respect

Rihana

From the Cartel with Love

Torn Between a Haitian Boss and a Jamaican Savage

She's got the Plug in his Feelings

Trap Wives of Charlotte 1-2

Tales of a Heaux

Caught up with a Mafia Boss 1-2

To Love a King

Tammi, Meek, and Cam: A Scandalous Love Affair 1-2

The Plug's Girl 1-2

A Bisset Cartel Love Story 1-2

Her Man Has My Heart

What You Know About Love

Cherished by a Thug

Enchanted: A Hood Love

A Savage Changed my Life

Bully and Envy: Love wasn't meant for a thug

Southern Bosses of North Carolina (Akai and Azalea)

Southern Bosses of Miami (Asa and Drew)

In Love with a Haitian Boss 1-2

Addicted to Mayhem: Loving the Plug

The Bugatti Boys